Ballroom Bedlam

Gunshots had erupted outside the building, and the crowd scrambled about in panic in the festive ballroom. Dodging between the well-dressed guests, Gary Manning saw a black-clad mercenary crouched among the box seats on the balcony. The sharp-eyed Canadian noticed that the merc carried an FAL rifle with the sling over his shoulder and that the man's arms moved, but the rifle didn't. Manning realized the merc had to be reaching for another weapon, and the Phoenix Force demolitions expert suspected what that might be.

He raised his Uzi machine pistol and aimed. He thumbed the selector lever to full auto to compensate for the reduced accuracy of the automatic weapon.

Manning triggered the SMG, and the parabellum slugs lashed the box seats. At least two rounds struck the mercenary in the head. As his body plummeted from view, Manning sighed with relief and lowered the Uzi.

The merc's grenade exploded a split second later.

Mack Bolan's

PHOENIX FORCE.

PHOENIX FORCE®

GAR WILSON

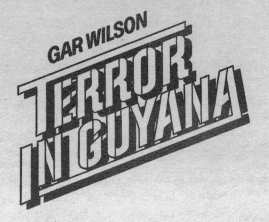

TERROR IN GUYANA

A GOLD EAGLE BOOK FROM
WORLDWIDE®

TORONTO · NEW YORK · LONDON · PARIS
AMSTERDAM · STOCKHOLM · HAMBURG
ATHENS · MILAN · TOKYO · SYDNEY

First edition May 1990

ISBN 0-373-61347-4

Special thanks and acknowledgment to
William Fieldhouse for his contribution to this work.

1

Gary Manning drove an uppercut to his opponent's stomach and followed with a left hook to the head. Thanks to his torso guard and helmet, Calvin James was spared the punishing force of the blows, but the attack still spun him about. He thrust his leg back in a variation of a karate side-kick and felt his foot connect. The padded slipper had struck Manning in the torso, and following up his advantage, James whipped a back-fist to his opponent's helmeted skull.

Manning's head was jarred by the blow. He grabbed James's arm with both hands before the black man could attack with another technique. He raised James's arm, yanked hard and ducked under it. Holding his opponent's wrist with one hand, he pulled it back as he shoved the other hand at James's elbow to lock the arm. James plunged forward and hurled into a somersault. Once again he crashed to the mat.

"Hold it!" Yakov Katzenelenbogen exclaimed as he stepped between the combatants. "Let's not get carried away with this contest. This is just a practice match. We don't want anyone to get hurt."

Middle-aged with short gray hair, intelligent eyes and a gentle, full mouth, Katz looked out of place dressed in a baggy gray sweat suit and tennis shoes. The steel hook of a prosthetic arm jutted from his right sleeve. Katz had lost the arm when he had served with the Israeli army during the Six Day War. That had been one of many wars he had survived in a remarkable career that spanned more than four decades.

"It's okay, Yakov," Manning assured him. "You're not hurt, are you, Cal?"

The black man got to his feet and managed a slight shrug despite the padded armor. "Not yet," he replied. "But I wouldn't mind if we call this one a draw."

"That's all right with me," Manning agreed. "What's the referee's verdict?"

"You both did well," Katz assured them. He fished a Timex watch from the pocket of his sweatshirt. "Let's hit the firing range for an hour or so. That'll be a good day's training all around."

"Fine with me," James confirmed as he removed his gloves. "I got a date tonight. You know what a date is? Been so long since I had one I had to look up what it means."

"Of course I know what a date is," Katz said in a serious voice. "It's a type of small edible fruit that grows on palm trees in the Middle East."

"Cute," James muttered as he slipped off his helmet. "You still see Julia once in a while, don't you?"

"Once in a while," Katz replied with a shrug. "She may be moving from Arlington soon. An institute for the blind in California has offered her a position as head of surgery. If she takes the job, I doubt that I'll see her at all. Between our work schedules and the added distance, I doubt the relationship will last."

Manning pulled off his helmet and looked at Katz. The older man tried to conceal his disappointment, but Manning realized Katz's feelings for Dr. Julia Kyler were deeper than he would admit even to himself. Katz had met Julia when he was hospitalized after being blinded by an explosion. They'd become romantically involved when he'd recovered his sight. For three years they had carried on a part-time relationship, but it seemed about to come to an end.

"I'm sorry, Yakov," Manning said sincerely.

"Well, it's been strained from the beginning," Katz stated. "Julia always knew I was involved in top secret operations for the federal government. She thinks it's CIA or the Justice Department. I've never been able to tell her any details, of course. It's hard for her to accept all the secrets I have to keep from her. She knows when I'm gone I may not be coming back, and she doesn't even know why. All things considered, she's been very patient and understanding."

James and Manning knew what Katz meant. Members of Phoenix Force, the ultra-secret five-man commando team, they had been selected from the best professional fighting men in the free world to serve in the special unit of the Stony Man operations. Trained in antiterrorism, espionage and virtually every form of combat, Phoenix Force was assigned the toughest missions that standard military, police and intelligence organizations could not handle.

"It's probably best for Julia if she makes a new start in California," Katz added. "She may have hoped that one day I'd retire from this business and we might have something that resembled a normal life together."

"Maybe you will some day," James commented.

"I've made too many enemies, Cal," Katz replied. "We all have. The past has a way of catching up with you. Even if I decided to retire, I'd be putting her life in danger if we stayed together. It's probably best this way."

"Maybe," Manning said, looking down at the floor. "But it can be lonely sometimes."

"I'm starting to feel guilty about having a date tonight," James said. "It'll be the first one in almost six months."

"That's one of the ironies about being with Phoenix Force," Manning remarked as he removed the pads from his torso and limbs. "We travel all over the world from Kenya to Antarctica and see a lot of things most people never will, but we sure don't have much of a social life. I suppose that's one of the sacrifices we have to make."

"Not tonight," James said with a grin. "Not for me, anyway. Just as long as I can get out of here by five o'clock so I can get ready for Olivia."

The report of pistol shots drew their attention to the door of the indoor firing range. The three Phoenix commandos had been working out in a *dojo*, or martial arts gymnasium. In addition to mats and full-contact protective gear, the *dojo* had a variety of equipment for physical training. *Makiwara* striking posts, wooden dummies with oak "limbs" and flexible rubber "heads" and ropes—strung through pulleys in the ceiling—with ankle straps for stretching leg muscles, were among the more exotic gear. There were also light punching bags, sets of weights and dumbbells, a rowing machine and other conventional equipment.

Rubber knives, phony pistols and rifles hung on the walls. These were used to practice disarming an armed opponent. The walls also displayed an assortment of unusual weapons and devices, including rock-maple fighting staves, chrome-plated *sai*, weighted chains, *nunchaku* fighting sticks, machetes and hatchets. The Phoenix Force commandos were not expert with all these weapons—some were more skilled with individual weapons than others—but all were familiar enough with the devices to use them in emergency combat.

"Sounds like our partners are already on the firing line," Manning commented. "We'd better join them before they burn up the firing range."

Inside the door, they took three Apache ear-protectors from a wall rack. Each man donned the ear-muff-style covers before entering the firing range portion of the Stony Man training center. Designed for pistols and submachine guns, the facility featured separate stalls and mechanically operated targets that traveled across a 125-yard range. An even larger indoor range was used for rifle practice.

Rafael Encizo stood at one stall, a blue-black pistol in his fists. Holding the gun in a two-handed Weaver's combat grip, the Cuban triggered three rounds at a silhouette target. He lowered the pistol, ejected a spent magazine from the butt-well and placed the gun on the bench. Although the slide was locked back and the chamber obviously empty, Encizo kept it pointed downrange. A fundamental rule of firearm safety is always to treat a weapon as if it is loaded and never point it at anything one does not intend to shoot.

As Encizo's three teammates joined him, he removed his Apache ear-protectors and greeted them. A well-muscled, very fit man with dark, handsome Latin features, Encizo did not look old enough to have participated in the Bay of Pigs invasion. Yet he was a veteran of this infamous paramilitary action, as well as dozens of other lesser-known operations, before joining Phoenix Force.

"We didn't see you in the *dojo*," James remarked. "Don't feel like going one-on-one at close quarters today?"

"I worked out for two hours in the gym and swam ten laps," Encizo replied. "Sorry if I sound like a wimp, but I'm over forty and I didn't feel like wrapping up the day by being bounced around on the mat. Besides, I was afraid I might get hit in the groin, and my plans for this evening might have been spoiled."

"You managed to get a date tonight, too?" Manning groaned. "I must be doing something wrong."

"If a social life is important to you, you'll find time for it," Encizo said with a smile. "Not much time, perhaps, but you just have to make the most of it."

"That's not the Walther we've been using," Katz commented as he looked at the pistol. "Is it one of the AT-88 autoloaders?"

"Yeah," Encizo confirmed with a nod.

The pistol was the full-sized AT-88S with adjustable sights and a barrel a little over four inches. It resembled the famous Czech CZ-75. The revolver-style trigger indicated it was a double-action autoloader. Imported from Switzerland, the AT-88 pistols were manufactured in three models that varied in size and capacity for ammunition. The most unique feature about the AT-88 line was its ability to fire either 9 mm cartridges or .41 Action Express ammo. The latter was a relatively new cartridge, developed several years earlier. The .41 A.E. round was sort of a cut-down version of a .41 Magnum cartridge. The 200-grain ammo with 955 f.p.s. velocity promised to be a formidable combat round.

"What do you think of it, Rafael?" Manning wanted to know.

"Well, I scored a pretty good shot group with it," Encizo replied, and tilted his head toward the target. The center of the silhouette had been chewed out by a number of close-set bullet holes. "I've actually done better with the Walther P-88 or the Heckler & Koch, but that might be because I'm more accustomed to those pistols. Still, for the first time with the AT-88, it handled pretty well."

"Did you shoot 9 mm or .41 Action Express?" James inquired.

"Forty-one A.E.," the Cuban answered. "Ten-round magazine. Of course, you have to change the barrels and magazines to fire 9 mm ammo. Then it handles fifteen rounds instead of ten."

"The 9 mm is an international cartridge available almost anywhere in the world," Katz commented. "The drawback on the .41 A.E. is that it's not plentiful, and we'd have trouble getting it abroad."

"I know," Encizo agreed. "But it might become a practical weapon for Phoenix Force if the caliber becomes more widely used and if the AT-88 proves to shoot both .41 A.E. and 9 mm well enough to rely on in combat."

"Have to carry out the tests another time, mates," a familiar voice announced from across the range.

The British accent, flavored with a Cockney twang, identified the voice as that of David McCarter. The fifth member of Phoenix Force was a tall, lean Briton with sly foxlike features and an unpredictable personality. His sweat suit looked particularly wrinkled, but his clothes always looked as if he had slept in them the night before. The butt of a Browning Hi-Power jutted from a shoulder holster under his left arm. McCarter stubbornly refused to part with the single-action autoloader, even though the other members of Phoenix Force carried double-action "Wondernine" Walthers. Since the Briton was an Olympic-level pistol marksman and remarkably accurate with the Browning, the others could not fault his decision.

"Hal wants to see us on the double," McCarter declared as he popped the tab from a chilled can of Coke. "I was over at the vending machines, minding my own business and getting a bit of harmless refreshment, when the in-house phone rang. Sure enough, it was the boss."

"Sounds like we have a mission," Katz remarked.

"Aw, man," James muttered. "Not tonight."

"Sorry, Cal," Manning told him with a sigh. "That's one of the most loathsome traits of terrorists—their timing really stinks."

HAL BROGNOLA WAITED for Phoenix Force in the Stony Man War Room. The middle-aged chief of operations always seemed exhausted, yet never appeared to run out of energy. This paradox was typical of Brognola. A veteran federal agent and law enforcement officer, he had dedicated his life to serving his country and protecting its people. Yet this man who believed so strongly in freedom had virtually surrendered his own in order to run Stony Man twenty-four hours a day.

The men of Phoenix Force wondered when Brognola had last enjoyed a full eight hours of sleep. The Fed ate meals while reading report files and computer printout sheets gathered from Intelligence sources throughout the world. He worked out assignments, cut through red tape and arranged liaisons with foreign governments and Intel case officers and agencies abroad. Brognola carried a tremendous burden of responsibility and a work load that would give most men a nervous breakdown within a month.

Brognola had been the head of operations since Stony Man began nearly ten years earlier. His only superior was the President of the United States. The man in the Oval Office, the only person who gave Brognola orders, actually knew few details about Stony Man or Phoenix Force. All he knew for certain was that the commando unit was successful and had yet to fail a mission, regardless of how big or difficult.

Brognola sat at the head of the conference table, a cigar stump clenched between his teeth. A stack of file folders and an onyx ashtray sat in front of the Fed. Phoenix Force took their seats and waited for Brognola to explain their newest assignment. McCarter leaned back in his chair and gulped down the last of his Coca Cola while Manning poured some coffee into a disposable cup.

"Sorry to hit you guys with another mission so soon after the last one," Brognola declared as he tapped the ash from his cigar. "I'm surprised I was lucky enough to catch all of you in the training center."

"Yeah," James said glumly. "We gotta stop hanging out there."

"We have to keep in training between missions," Katz stated as he took a pack of Camel cigarettes from his sweatshirt pocket. "So, what's the job, Hal?"

"I'm sure all of you remember Reverend Jim Jones and the Guyana massacre?" Brognola inquired. The Fed opened a folder as he spoke.

"Will anybody forget it?" James replied. "Jones had set up a commune for his People's Temple religious sect in Guyana. A California congressman named Leo Ryan went down there to investigate claims that Jones was running a kind of terror cult with people held in check by armed guards, public beatings and lots of threats. I remember the stories real well at the time because I was a San Francisco cop back then. The People's Temple once had its headquarters in Frisco. It still had an active church in the city when news broke of the murders and mass suicides in Guyana.''

Manning took over. ''Congressman Ryan and some journalists were shot to death, and more than nine hundred members of Jones's cult committed suicide. They lined up and drank a fruit drink laced with cyanide. I think Jones shot himself in the head. Only a few People's Temple followers managed to escape.''

''The incident made headlines all over the world,'' Encizo remarked, ''but that was more than ten years ago, Hal.''

''November 1978,'' Brognola confirmed. He handed the folder to Katz. ''However, these photographs were taken less than twenty-four hours ago.''

Katz examined the photos. The scene was all too familiar to the Phoenix Force commander. Bodies were sprawled across the ground by a small village. Men, women and children lay lifeless, twisted in unnatural positions. Hands were frozen in death grips at chests and throats. Faces were contorted by fear and pain. Katz had seen such carnage many times before. The setting was different, yet the scene revived images of a massacre long ago, when Nazi storm troopers slaughtered a youthful Yakov Katzenelenbogen's family and neighbors in a Jewish ghetto in Europe.

''How did this happen?'' Katz inquired as he passed the folder and photographs to Manning.

''Autopsies of the dead showed that they died from cyanide poisoning,'' Brognola replied. ''Remains of liquid in the stomach confirm that it was administered by drinking a cherry-flavored non-carbonated drink. The massacre occurred in Guyana, and it's being labeled as a 'mass suicide under suspicious circumstances.' It's like the People's Temple all over again.''

"Not quite," Manning declared. "Most of the people in these photos are dressed like East Indians, and the others look like teenaged Americans. I don't claim to know much about the People's Temple, but it seemed to me the majority of followers were poor blacks from the United States."

"And Jones was a Christian minister, more or less," James added. "He started as a Methodist in the early fifties but gradually developed a more cultlike congregation. His so-called religion leaned more toward Marxism and personal control of his followers than anything connected with Bible teachings. But none of his followers were Hindus."

"You're right," Brognola assured him. "The villagers in these photographs were of East Indian descent. They were Hindus, not Christians. They had set up a communal farming village, but I doubt any of them were Marxist. Apparently the villagers never gave a damn about politics one way or the other. We don't have much information so far, but all evidence suggests it was just a quiet, peaceful little hamlet with a few farming families who grew crops largely for their own use and sold the rest at nearby towns."

"How many were killed?" Encizo asked grimly as he looked at the photos.

"Forty-nine, total," the Fed answered, "including the American kids in the photos. The two Jeeps in some of the shots have been traced to a rental agency in Georgetown. Robert Albert Handel signed for them with his credit card. You may not know Bobby Handel, but you may have heard of his father, Senator Theodore Handel of Illinois."

"I'm still a British citizen, you know," McCarter said. "Can't expect me to keep up with all these blokes involved in American politics."

"Hey, I'm from Chicago originally," James declared. "I still have some interest in what goes on in Illinois and who gets elected to office, although I haven't been back to the Windy City for years. I remember when Handel ran for office. Pretty much campaigned as an old-fashioned liberal and made a lot of promises about how great everything would be if he got in the U.S. Senate. I'm not even sure what the guy was before they elected him to the Senate: congressman or state senator or head dogcatcher in Springfield, something like that. As far as I know, he hasn't done diddly-shit since he got into the senate."

"Typical," Encizo snorted. The Cuban was even more cynical about politics than James. "Politicians are all professional liars who will say anything to get elected, do whatever benefits them and their cronies. After that, they lie through their teeth all over again to get reelected."

"Democracy in action," Manning said dryly. "So this dullard senator's kid is among the victims in Guyana?"

"His body isn't among the dead," Brognola explained. "Neither is the body of his girlfriend, Lynn Carlston, who went to Guyana with him. Apparently the Handel kid was the head of a group of volunteers who went to South America to help the poor and needy."

"We got poor and needy here in the United States," James growled. "It would be nice if some of these do-gooders would concentrate on doing good here before we export all that charity to other countries."

"Don't be too hard on the Handel kid, Cal," the Fed urged. "From what we've got on him, he was involved in all sorts of activities to help the homeless, raise money for

AIDS research, protect the environment and oppose injustice and corruption both here and abroad. In short, he was young and idealistic. There are worse things to be.''

"You said 'he *was*,'" Manning observed. "If his body wasn't found at the village, he might still be alive."

"That's what Senator Handel hopes, too," Brognola replied. "The senator thinks his son may have been grabbed for ransom. He's been demanding, pleading and almost begging the President to help him get his son back. Apparently Handel feels sort of guilty about what happened to Bob because he arranged to send him to Guyana."

"Why?" Encizo asked. "Since the Jonestown incident, people have just forgotten Guyana even exists. If they do think of it, they're usually recalling what happened with Jim Jones and the People's Temple."

"Right," the Fed agreed. "There haven't been any violent revolutions or serious human rights violations reported in Guyana—although there has been some doubt about how fair the elections are down there."

"You can say the same thing about Cook County," James muttered.

"The point is, Guyana is about as volatile as the state of Idaho," Brognola explained. "Which, by the way, is just about the same size as Guyana, but with a larger population. Handel figured he could send his son down there to get him out of the United States for a while. Bobby was embarrassing daddy by participating in all those protests and demonstrations. Kid got himself arrested and stirred up some trouble among party leaders in Chicago when he discovered a local captain of industry was dumping toxic waste illegally."

"Now, that sounds familiar," James remarked. "I just didn't remember it was Handel's son. So, the old man sent him down to Guyana because he figured he wouldn't get in any trouble there?''

"That's about the size of it," Brognola confirmed. "So the President wants you guys to go to Guyana and find out what the hell happened. If Bob Handel is still alive, the President wants you to bring him back to the States. He also wants to find out who's responsible for the newest fatal fruit drink party. It's hard to imagine that that peaceful little village of Hindu farmers would suddenly commit mass suicide exactly as Jim Jones's cult did over a decade ago. And who can believe that the Americans went along with it because they politely wanted to follow local customs?''

"What about the People's Temple?" Katz inquired. "The cult still has followers. True, it was all but wiped out, but there are still a few hard-core members in the U.S. Did any of those American volunteers belong to the cult? Is a branch still active in Guyana?''

"Aaron is trying to get information on those questions right now," Brognola assured him. "At this point we don't have any idea who did it or why. All we know for certain is that forty-nine people are dead, and it seems pretty senseless. The whole world will know within a few hours, so you can expect to see a small army of reporters and TV camera crews running around down there. That won't make your job any easier.''

"The press always flocks to a story with a lot of interest to the public," McCarter commented as he gazed down at the photographs. "And everybody loves a good horror story. Even if it's a rerun of one ten years old.''

2

"Was it necessary?" Karin Weissflog asked quietly, unable to look at her husband's face.

Otto Weissflog sat at his desk in the den and polished the three-foot blade of his saber. He glanced at his wife. She was forty years old, yet her clear complexion and wide blue eyes reminded him of the young "milkmaid" girl he had married twenty years earlier. Karin's blond hair was tied in a bun with braids bound around it like a golden crown. She dressed in a modest housedress with a high white collar and a long hem that almost touched her slippers. Karin was a personification of a proper German wife, a Teutonic goddess and earth mother. To Otto Weissflog, she was still the perfect woman.

"Why was what necessary?" Weissflog inquired, although he knew what she was talking about.

"I listen to the radio, Otto," Karin told him. "The news about the village is a major story. Did you have to do it?"

"The village was a mass suicide," he said as he slid the saber into its scabbard, which bore a two-inch black swastika on either side. "Isn't that how the newscast describes it?"

"A *suspected* mass suicide," Karin replied. "They are comparing it to that terrible incident in Jonestown."

"Jonestown was hardly a tragedy," Weissflog insisted. "Negroes and American white trash—and I'm sure none of them were pure Caucasians. The United States is even more racially corrupted by Jews and blacks and other inferiors than Europe or even South America. When those subhuman garbage killed themselves in 1978, it was probably the only worthwhile action in their entire worthless lives."

"I've heard this so many times before," Karin said sadly as she shook her head. "My father, your father, you and so many others. They were still people, Otto. They may not be our racial equals, but they are still people and please do not change the subject. We're not talking about what happened at Jonestown. We're talking about what happened yesterday."

"It's better if you don't know certain things, Karin," he replied, rising from his chair. "All I can say is we are fighting a kind of shadowy war, and all wars claim casualties."

Carrying the saber, he crossed the room and hung the sword diagonally across another saber already mounted on the wall. Weissflog's den was decorated with dozens of weapons. Most were German and Austrian. Some were very old, such as the matching pair of eighteenth-century Austrian military officers' sabers and several halberds, lances and maces. Others were mementos of World Wars I and II. A "Broomhandle" Mauser pistol, two Lugers and an MP-40 Schmeisser submachine gun were mounted in glass cases. Several styles of bayonets and grenades were also displayed.

Two German helmets and a black service cap with Gestapo insignia were mounted on the shelf of a bookcase above a row of leather-bound books in English and German. These included works by the leaders of the German National Socialist Party of the 1930s and 1940s—the despised Nazis. Feder and Rosenberg with their views on economics, sociology and racial purity were represented in his bookcase. Eckart's *Bolshevism from Moses to Lenin* concentrated on "proving" the Jews were a horrendous threat to Western Europe. The most honored book in Weissflog's collection was *Mein Kampf* by Adolf Hitler.

"What kind of war are you fighting that demands killing innocent farmers?" Karin asked. "Old men, women and children are dead!"

"During the war, the British and the Americans bombed Dresden without mercy and they didn't care how many German civilians were killed in the process," Weissflog told her. "They didn't shed any tears for the 'innocent lives' lost at Hiroshima and Nagasaki when atomic bombs were dropped on those cities. What are forty-nine nonwhite and non-Christian savages and some American race-mixers compared to the thousands claimed by those military actions of the past?"

"I've always stood by you, Otto," Karin said. "I always will, but I can't help feeling upset by this."

"I'm sorry you found out about it," Weissflog said sincerely. "I assure you, it was necessary. In the end, what we accomplish will be worth everything we must do now."

The telephone on Weissflog's desk rang. Relieved by the interruption, he hurried to the phone, bumping into a brass umbrella stand in his haste. A Bavarian walking stick and an Austrian hiker's stave rattled in the stand. Weissflog picked up the phone. It was an in-house line, so he spoke his real name into the mouthpiece.

"Guten Morgen, Mein Herr," Werner's voice declared. He always spoke German whenever the opportunity arose. "Your guests have arrived."

"Sehr gut, danke," Weissflog replied. "Very good, thank you. I'm in the den. Bring them to me."

"Ja, Mein Herr," Werner said, a trace of distaste in his voice. "Just please do not ask me to touch either of them."

"I know it is loathsome to have to deal with such men," Weissflog said with a sigh. "But it is necessary, and you must be polite to them. Understand?"

"Ich verstehe," Werner assured him.

Weissflog hung up and turned to his wife. Karin nodded, aware that she had to leave, and departed. Weissflog moved behind the desk, took a seat, opened a drawer and removed a Walther P-38 pistol. It had been his father's gun. The old man had given it to him a few months before he died.

Weissflog would never forget his father's last days. Frail, wasted by age and cancer, the old man lay helpless in his bed until he finally gasped his last breath. His father had been Weissflog's mentor and role model. His entire education and beliefs had come from his father's teachings. Weissflog had regarded his father as a god. When the god had died, Weissflog vowed to continue his father's work in Guyana.

Captain Gerhard Weissflog had been an officer in the Amt/Ausland mit der Oberkommando der Wehrmacht—better known as the Abwehr. The Foreign Department of the Military High Command during Hitler's regime had started a secret campaign in South America as early as 1938. The Abwehr concentrated on building a "fifth column" in Brazil, but Captain Weissflog's assignment had been to set up a smaller, covert operation in British Guiana. One of the first soldiers trained as a "Werewolf," Captain Weissflog was an elite commando as well as an espionage agent. The Werewolves were a special unit, fluent in English and adept in sabotage, codes and communications, small arms and hand-to-hand combat.

Many of the Werewolves were a disappointment. Their English was thickly accented, and they failed to convince anyone they were really British or American soldiers when dropped behind enemy lines. However, Gerhard Weissflog had spent much of his childhood in England and had been raised with two languages. He had been a perfect choice for the Abwehr's plan in British Guiana. The captain assumed the identity of a murdered British citizen and traveled to South America in 1940. With the enormous funds of the Third Reich to finance his mission, Weissflog set himself up as a respectable businessman and plantation owner in British Guiana.

However, by 1942 it was obvious the Nazi schemes in South America were failing. Abwehr operations in Brazil fell apart after President Vargas's chief of police, a Nazi sympathizer named Filinto Muller, was removed from office and British Intelligence and the American FBI were closing in on German spy rings. Argentina became the center of Nazi espionage in South America by 1943, but the proverbial handwriting was already on the wall. The Axis powers were losing the covert war in South America, and soon it was obvious Hitler's forces were being beaten on other fronts throughout the world. Admiral Wilhelm Canaris, the head of Abwehr, was executed in March 1945 by the SS for alleged involvement in the conspiracy to assassinate Hitler the year before. Two months later, Hitler himself was dead and the Third Reich surrendered.

Weissflog had not been detected. He continued living under his assumed identity and secretly contacted Nazis hiding in other South American countries. The war was over, and Captain Weissflog could have simply gone home and reclaimed his old life. He had been part of Hitler's Final Solution, which involved the slaughter of millions of Jews, Slavs and other "undesirables." The captain had never participated in torturing prisoners, political assassination or any other activity that would have placed him on the list of "war criminals." Yet he believed in the Third Reich and everything Adolf Hitler stood for. The war was not over for Gerhard Weissflog.

His son, born in 1950, was raised and educated on the "Wilkens's plantation." As an infant, Otto Weissflog was fed Nazi propaganda as if it was mother's milk. His parents and surrogate uncles were all Nazis. His teachers and nannies were Nazis, and his playmates were the sons and daughters of Nazis. Otto Weissflog's mental and emotional conditioning for devotion to the beliefs, prejudices and ambitions of National Socialism and Adolf Hitler was even greater than that of his father, because it started at birth. The extremist notions of the fugitive Nazi veterans were the only doctrines he was exposed to until he was thirteen.

However, the world was changing beyond the plantation. British Guiana was granted the right to self-government. It became an independent nation and restored its traditional name of Guyana in 1966, and finally declared itself a republic without ties to Great Britain in 1970, although it remained a member of the Commonwealth. The prime ministers of Guyana represented different political parties, but all were East Indians or blacks. It was ironic that Weissflog and his fellow Nazis were forced to hide in a country ruled by men they felt belonged to racially inferior species. It was a bitter pill for the fanatics to swallow.

The Nazis were also worried about the growing influence of communism in Central America, which was threatening to spread to the south. The election of Salvador Allende Gossens as president of Chile in 1970 terrified them because Allende was openly a Marxist-Leninist. They were relieved when Allende was overthrown three years later by a military coup, even though the Sandinista leftists took control of Nicaragua after Somoza fled the country in 1979. Communism remained a serious concern for the Nazis.

They were even more concerned about the threat of being hunted down by Israeli agents. Adolf Eichmann had been captured in Argentina in 1960 and stood trial in Israel. He was hanged in 1962. Klaus Barbie was taken to France to stand trial for war crimes, and other Nazi fugitives were being stalked by government agencies and determined individuals. Such events gave the Nazis more reason for nightmares.

Captain Weissflog had died without seeing the Third Reich rise again, but his son intended to continue in his father's footsteps. At long last, he believed the time was right to carry out his scheme. However, the task would require the assistance of allies whom his late father never would have considered.

OTTO WEISSFLOG WORKED the slide to his Walther P-38 and chambered the first round. He slipped on the safety and returned the pistol to the desk drawer. The Nazi had no reason to believe his visitors would be foolish enough to attempt any act of violence within the compound, but he regarded them as subhuman and thus half-savage. They had to be considered uncivilized and unpredictable, in Weissflog's opinion, so he prepared for the worst.

Werner and Reinhard escorted the guests into the den. Each of the pair resembled the other enough to be a brother. Both were large, thickly muscled with barrel chests and massive shoulders. Their jaws were heavy, and their Nordic blue eyes were set close together. Each wore his hair clipped short, emphasizing their thick bull necks and broad rugged faces. Werner was two inches shorter than Reinhard, and his nose had been broken on three occasions, which left it slightly crooked at the bridge. Otherwise it would be difficult to tell the men apart.

Weissflog had known Werner and Reinhard since childhood. They had been born in a Nazi stronghold in Paraguay, the sons of former SS officers who had fled to South America after the war. Werner and Reinhard were pure Aryan stock, physically powerful, fanatically dedicated and loyal to Weissflog. The Nazi commander trusted them more than anyone except Karin and his own son, Gerhart. They were his personal aides and bodyguards. Weissflog had no doubt they would willingly sacrifice their lives before they would let any harm befall him or his family.

The visitors did not look as if they would be willing guests at a Nazi stronghold—except possibly as human guinea pigs for medical experiments of the sort that concentration-camp butchers with names like Mengele, Grawitz, Schumann and Gebhardt had carried out on Jews, gypsies, Slavs and other prisoners in the name of scientific research. More recently, before it was destroyed by a mysterious commando strike, a New Order Nazi stronghold in the Amazon headed by Kurt Mohn, had used Indians from jungle tribes for experiments to test a synthetic virus for use as a biochemical weapon.

François Guillotin and Captain Ajmer were willing visitors at Weissflog's home because they were co-conspirators in his cause.

A tall, muscular Haitian black man, Guillotin had formerly been a member of Duvalier's infamous Ton Ton Macoute secret police. He wore a short-sleeved white shirt and gold-rimmed sunglasses—an unofficial trademark of the Haitian goon squad.

Ajmer was six inches shorter, heavyset, with brown skin and eyes that slanted at the folds, revealing his Tibeto-Mongolian bloodline. Ajmer was a Gurkha warrior from Nepal. He wore a khaki uniform with canvas boots and a *kukri* fighting knife in a buffalo-horn scabbard on his belt. Ajmer had refused to surrender the big, curve-bladed knife, although he agreed to hand over his British Webley revolver before entering the den. Werner and Reinhard watched the pair with suspicion and kept a special watch on the burly Gurkha.

"Well, gentlemen," Weissflog began, forcing a slight smile. He hated the fact that two representatives of what he considered "inferior races" were in his den, yet he needed their help. "I trust you've prepared your men, and they're ready to begin their assignments."

"We do our job," Guillotin replied in a nasal, heavily accented voice. French Creole was his native tongue. The accent grated on Weissflog's ear.

"As long as we get paid," Ajmer added. His accent was almost British, clipped and precise, yet slightly singsong as if reciting a limerick that failed to rhyme.

"You're being well paid," said Weissflog. "I didn't expect mercenaries to have any sense of loyalty unless it served to make a profit."

Guillotin chuckled and shook his head. "I am not an expert in the philosophy of the Nazi Party," he stated.

"But I know enough to realize you regard people of my skin color as little more than monkeys. If I am going to help a bigot seize power, I think I deserve to be very well paid indeed."

Werner and Reinhard stiffened. Both seemed ready to reach for their side arms. But Weissflog gestured to them to let the remark pass. He looked at Guillotin and shrugged.

"You think what you like of me," Weissflog declared. "I really don't care as long as you do your job. However, I am aware of your past, Mr. Guillotin—although I suspect that's not your real name. You used to be referred to as 'the Guillotine' when you were with the Ton Ton Macoute in Haiti. Isn't that why you assumed the name of the inventor of that famous French instrument of execution?"

"One name is as good as another," Guillotin replied.

"Perhaps," Weissflog allowed with a slight smile. "However, you earned the title 'the Guillotine' because of your expertise at chopping off hands and heads with a machete. Your blade descended on the wrists and necks of dozens of your fellow Haitians. The Ton Ton Macoute had a well-deserved reputation for ruthlessness and brutality. I understand you killed peasants for entertainment. Gunned them down and beat them to death in broad daylight and in front of witnesses because you knew you were above the law."

"We *were* the law," Guillotin insisted. "You can see what has happened to Haiti since we were forced to flee the country. Chaos and anarchy have replaced law and order."

"I suppose a person wouldn't disobey any laws after you chop his head off," Weissflog scoffed. "My point is, you're hardly qualified to criticize the morality of the

Nazi Party. You've killed far more of your black brothers than I have.''

''I've had more opportunities,'' the Haitian said with a frosty grin. ''I'm sure you will surpass my body count in time.''

Weissflog shrugged. Captain Ajmer grunted with annoyance. The Gurkha mercenary didn't care about the color of his opponents or the politics and prejudices of his employer. To Ajmer, people fit four categories: his fellow mercenaries under his command, his present employer, the targets he was paid to hit and the innocent bystanders who happened to be in the right place at the wrong time. The last category of people he regarded as extras in a movie. Usually they were just in the way. Occasionally they became targets because they sided against the mercs.

Ajmer's simple sense of morality did not extend beyond the small group of Gurkhas, Nepalese and Tamils in his mercenary army. His ancestors had been great warriors who once fought the British in the great Gurkha War of 1814 to 1816. Others served in the elite Gurkha Regiments in the British colonies in India. Ajmer had been born to warrior stock. Nepal was not about to go to war with India or Tibet, and the British colonies in India were gone. He chose the profession that allowed him to fight wars, choose his own battlefields and got paid far better than an average soldier.

''My men are prepared to carry out their mission,'' he declared, ''but I want to pay them again before they go into the field.''

''They were already paid,'' Werner snorted sourly.

''We were paid when we first arrived in Guyana six months ago,'' Ajmer replied, addressing Weissflog. ''They haven't been able to spend much of it, but they want the next installment of their pay in order to feel more secure. Believe it or not, we've had clients who have tried to cheat us. In Sri Lanka, three years ago, for example, a Sinhalese official hired us to handle a Tamil guerrilla uprising, then refused to pay and threatened to have the army arrest us."

Ajmer touched the handle of his *kukri* knife. He added, "The official woke up one morning and discovered blood on his bedsheets by his mistress. When he tried to wake her, he found her head had been cut from her body and placed back at the stump of her neck. He also discovered one third of his guards had been decapitated in the night. No one heard a thing. No one knew how we got in and killed so many so silently. The Sinhalese aren't Gurkhas, so they don't understand how we become shadows in the night. Needless to say, the official decided to pay us after that."

"How dare you threaten us!" Reinhard snapped, eyes wide with anger.

The bodyguards were ready to draw their pistols. Ajmer seemed unconcerned, as if confident he could draw his *kukri* fast enough to cut down both men before either could use his side arm. Weissflog was getting aggravated with all four of the men.

"Stop it!" the Nazi leader snapped. "This is foolish! There is no need for veiled threats or absurd gestures of courage that are meant only to impress or intimidate. Captain Ajmer's request for payment is perfectly acceptable. Soldiers—even patriotic soldiers—expect to be paid. We're all students of military history. Surely we all know enough to realize any army that didn't pay its soldiers has failed. It's important for morale, and if the soldiers aren't paid, they are apt to pillage and steal to make some sort of profit. Payment is even more important to mercenaries who are not patriots.''

"My men aren't patriots," Ajmer admitted. "They're professionals. They carry out their missions with precise skill and without any emotional baggage to interfere with their success. That's exactly what you need for this operation to work, Mr. Wilkens.''

"You'll receive the next pay installment today," Weissflog announced. He glanced from Ajmer to Guillotin as he spoke. "You will *all* be paid. Just make certain there are no mistakes.''

"The only mistakes will be made by anyone who tries to stop us," the Gurkha assured him.

3

Timehri International Airport, the largest in Guyana, was tiny compared to most major airports in the United States, Europe or South America. Still, it was relatively modern and efficient; a far cry from the caricatured image of a banana republic airline with rickety old twin-engined craft and passengers sharing seats with chickens and pigs.

Phoenix Force arrived at Timehri International in the late afternoon. They deplaned from a C-130 transport, which landed at a runway near the farthest row of hangars from the main terminal. The U.S. military plane allowed the commandos to bypass inspections and customs officials in the States. The Guyanese government had arranged similar waivers.

Three men waited by a small gray bus parked near a hangar. The national flag of Guyana—a green banner bisected by two triangles, a red pyramid superimposed on a yellow one—was attached to the radio antenna of the bus. Two of the men by the bus wore khaki uniforms that revealed British influence. The taller of the pair appeared to be of East Indian descent and wore a maroon *pagris*, or turban, instead of a cap or beret. The other soldier was a thin black man dressed in a long camouflage-print field jacket and a maroon beret.

The third man was a short, portly figure dressed in a single-breasted suit, white shirt and striped tie. A white man, he appeared to be in his mid-forties. Phoenix Force recognized this man as a CIA case officer named George Sutcliffe. They had read a personnel file on Sutcliffe and knew he was actually in his late thirties and had been stationed at the U.S. Embassy in Georgetown for the last two years.

Phoenix Force hauled their luggage from the plane. The commando team carried aluminum suitcases, long, narrow rifle cases and briefcases. They were dressed in casual clothing, but all wore jackets or windbreakers in spite of the tropical climate. Beneath the loose-fitting garments, the bulge of pistols in shoulder leather under armpits was barely noticeable.

"I'm Sutcliffe," the CIA man announced as he approached the commandos. "I believe you've been told I'd meet you here."

"Don't you want to see our passports?" Katz inquired dryly. Sutcliffe was supposed to ask for their passports as a password to identify himself and assure them that everything was going according to plan.

"Oh, that?" Sutcliffe scoffed, shaking his head. "This is Guyana, not East Germany. Let's not be melodramatic."

"Or careless," Rafael Encizo replied. "You'd better be taking this mission seriously, Sutcliffe."

"Of course I take this seriously," the CIA man said, clearly offended. "You men have White House authority, so I'm well aware—"

"Let's not discuss this out here," Katz said sharply. The Israeli was always security-conscious and had developed a sense of professional paranoia.

"Better if we talk in the bus," the Indian soldier declared.

No one argued. They loaded their gear into the vehicle. Sutcliffe watched Manning and Encizo take transistor radios from their briefcases, raise the antennae and switch them on. The others sat in the bus and waited for the Canadian and Cuban to join them. Both men nodded and climbed into the vehicle.

"Bug sweep?" Sutcliffe asked. "We already checked for electronic listening devices."

"It doesn't hurt to double-check," Manning told him.

The "transistor radios" were really detecting devices used to locate hidden microphones and transmitters. If such eavesdropping instruments had been present, the "radios" would have sounded a soft beeping that would have grown louder as the antennae got closer to the bug.

The black Guyanese slipped behind the steering wheel and started the engine. The bus rolled forward and headed for an exit gate. Sutcliffe looked at the rifle cases and shook his head. The CIA man didn't have to voice his thoughts. Phoenix Force knew what was going through Sutcliffe's mind. He was wondering what kind of lunatic cowboys the White House had sent to investigate the incident in Guyana.

"Oh, this is Lieutenant Colonel Barama," Sutcliffe announced as he gestured toward the East Indian Guyanese. "The officer at the wheel is Captain Takutu. They're with the Guyana Defense Forces, attached to the ministry of national security."

"Welcome to my country," Barama said with a curt bow. "I wish the circumstances of your visit were different. We have been instructed by the prime minister himself to assist you in any way necessary in your investigation."

"We're not primarily criminal investigators," Katz explained. "Our primary job is direct action, but first we have to locate a target and make absolutely certain it's the right one. The information we have so far isn't much help. Have you been able to come up with any additional data?"

"I'm not certain what you've been told so far," the colonel admitted. "You know about the village and alleged mass suicide. We believe it's probably murder. There were tire tracks that did not fit those of the Americans' Jeeps. The other vehicles were British Land Rovers. We also found horse hoofprints. There were no horses in the village."

"That's a start," Calvin James remarked. "Were all the victims poisoned in the same manner?"

"Most drank the poisoned drink," Barama explained. "Some had been injected with cyanide by syringe. We found three syringes at the village. No fingerprints on any of them."

"Pretty odd that anybody who commits suicide would wipe off the syringes before they died," David McCarter commented as he drummed his fingers on the attaché case on his lap. "This might be a stupid question, but have you got any idea what happened to the Handel kid and his girlfriend?"

"No," Barama replied with a sigh. "However, to be honest, we have little experience with such investigations, and the news reporters arrived almost as fast as we did. Keeping them away from the scene has required more manpower than we've been able to give to the investigation itself."

"Terrific," Manning muttered with disgust.

"The press is giving the Guyanese authorities a hard time about this," Sutcliffe stated. "They're screaming accusations of cover ups and attempts to repress the truth. They don't appreciate the fact that the investigators have to keep them at bay because they'll trample all over the crime scene and destroy evidence.''

''Yeah, I can sympathize,'' Calvin James, the ex-cop, declared. ''How'd the press get here so fast?''

''A pair of merchants from Tumatumari found the bodies when they arrived at the village to purchase coconuts and vegetables to sell at the market,'' Barama explained. ''One of them saw this as an opportunity to get paid for giving a news story to journalists. Mostly foreigners in Venezuela. Americans, British, Venezuelans themselves. It didn't take long for them to arrive. Unfortunately we haven't been able to complete our investigation for that reason.''

''Looks like we're starting from square one,'' Encizo said with a shrug. ''Maybe that's just as well. If you've been able to keep the news hounds from stomping the evidence into oblivion, maybe we can find some clues to what happened.''

''Well, the colonel has his own theory,'' the CIA officer said, glancing at Barama.

''We'd certainly like to hear it,'' Katz said.

''It is not my theory, but one endorsed by the minister of national security,'' Colonel Barama began. ''He believes the recent massacre was the work of the same group responsible for the original massacre a dozen years ago.''

''The People's Temple?'' James asked with surprise.

Barama nodded solemnly as the bus rolled along the road to Georgetown. The traffic was light as dusk descended and a blanket of twilight fell across the sky. The streetlights turned on. The scent of the salty Atlantic rode on a breeze from the north through the coastal town.

Guyana's capital resembled an oversized town transplanted from New England. Rows of small wooden houses and a few larger buildings stood between grassy lawns and miniature parks. Yet the pleasant setting suddenly changed as flames erupted from a building near the edge of the city. Figures rushed through the street as the bus rolled into Georgetown.

"Good grief!" Sutcliffe exclaimed, eyes wide with astonishment. "What the hell happened?"

"Looks like a riot," Encizo replied as he peered out at the chaos outside the vehicle.

DOZENS OF PEOPLE DARTED from the burning structure and other nearby buildings. Flames danced from shattered windows. Harsh yellow light flickered across the angry figures in the street. Blacks and Indians confronted one another armed with an assortment of improvised weapons—rakes, hoes, axe handles, chains, rocks, knives. The combatants were of two ethnic groups, each fighting the other.

Voices shouted angry challenges and threats in at least three languages. Sticks clashed as opponents tried to bash the other's head in. Some clubs struck victims. Shapes wilted to the ground, assaulted by frenzied blows. Rocks and bricks were hurled in all directions across more than two city blocks. Rioters threw projectiles at the bus and other vehicles.

Phoenix Force and their companions saw the burning building more clearly as the bus drew closer to the conflict. It was a church, two stories high, with an eight-foot steeple. Flames crackled along the windowsills and licked the roof. The church was made of wood and burned rapidly despite the frenzied efforts of a handful of black

men, women and children who tried to extinguish the
blaze with buckets of water and a small garden hose.

Stones banged on the roof of the bus and smashed a
spider-web pattern of cracks in the windshield. A brick
shattered the front window on the passenger side. Captain Takutu, who had been driving, cried out when a
shard of glass flew into his face and pierced his cheek just
below his eye. A trio of rioters charged into the middle of
the street and lobbed more projectiles at the bus. Takutu
had stomped on the gas pedal to speed away. Although
highly excited, he swerved the bus sharply to avoid the
rioters in the streets.

The vehicle swung to the right. One person refused to
go without delivering a final attack on the bus. He
launched himself at the side of the bus and slammed a
club against the metal body of the rig. The tail of the bus
caught him on the right hip, knocking him across the
pavement in a clumsy cartwheel.

Takutu managed to avoid other rioters, but he steered
the bus into the metal post of a street lamp. The grill
crunched and the hood popped open. Steaming water
spilled from the ruptured radiator. The passengers violently bounced within the vehicle as it came to an abrupt
halt.

"Oh, my God!" Sutcliffe gasped as he gripped his
sprained neck and watched the rioters in fear.

A frenzied group detached itself from the rest of the
mob and headed for the crippled vehicle. Some pelted the
bus with rocks and bricks as they approached. Others,
their eyes filled with rage and terror, wielded blunt instruments and knives. They lashed out blindly, barely
aware of their target. The men who descended on the bus
were black Guyanese, but the Indian rioters seemed to be
equally consumed by madness.

"I think we should reason with these blokes," Mc-Carter declared as he kicked open the emergency door at the rear of the bus.

The British commando jumped from the exit. He landed about two yards from a tall wiry black man who screamed like a banshee, charged, and swung an axe handle at McCarter's head. The Briton dropped to one knee and ducked. He heard the axe strike the bus.

McCarter drove a fist between his attacker's legs. The rioter wheezed breathlessly at the blow to his genitals. Jumping up, the Briton smashed a forearm under the rioter's wrists, knocking the club toward the sky. Mc-Carter grabbed the handle and twisted it from the Guyanese's grasp. The rioter's mouth hung open, and his eyes squeezed shut from the agony between his legs.

The British commando shoved the man aside, aware that he was fully immobilized. The Guyanese fell to his knees. A second rioter tripped over the fallen figure, while a third attacked McCarter with a garden hoe. The Briton swung the axe handle into the shaft of his opponent's weapon. Wood met wood and the impact rode through the handle into McCarter's fists and arms. He kicked his attacker's ribs and chopped the axe handle across the man's chest to knock the rioter backward into other frenzied assailants.

Another rioter, a butcher knife in his fist, attempted to grab McCarter from behind. Calvin James suddenly emerged from the bus. The bad-ass from Chicago swung a kick to the knifeman's abdomen. Fixed on McCarter, the Guyanese failed to notice James until the Phoenix pro lashed a boot into his gut.

As soon as James's foot touched the ground, he pivoted and delivered a roundhouse kick with his other leg. The butcher knife went hurtling from the rioter's fingers. James punched the guy in the face, and he stumbled backward, dazed. The tough American unleashed a side-kick to the man's chest and sent him tumbling into another pair of rioters.

A rampaging Guyanese, armed with a short piece of pipe, charged James. As he ducked, James drew a Blackmoor Dirk from a sheath clipped under his right arm. He slashed the six-inch, double-edged blade across the opponent's forearm, above the hand holding the pipe. The rioter screamed and dropped his weapon. James followed the knife stroke with a solid right cross to the man's jaw, then chopped the bottom of his fist under his opponent's heart. The blow drove the guy backward and dropped him to the ground on his rump. Dazed and winded, the rioter seemed more concerned with the possibility of bleeding to death from the gash in his arm than with trying to continue the fight.

Emerging from the side door of the bus, Gary Manning confronted two rioters. One, holding a heavy wooden two-by-four, tried to use the board as a battering ram on the vehicle. The other wielded an iron chain in one fist and a claw hammer in the other. The Canadian grunted with displeasure as the guy with the battering ram launched a vicious attack, aiming it at Manning's stomach, apparently intending to reduce the Canadian's belly to pulp.

Sidestepping his attacker, Manning hit him with a hard left hook. He grabbed the board with both hands as the man's head bounced. He shoved the beam into its owner and pushed him at the rioter armed with the chain.

Iron links lashed out and struck flesh. The guy with the two-by-four moaned. Half the chain was wrapped around his head. His comrade gasped when he realized he had flogged his friend with the chain. Manning yanked the beam from his dazed opponent and swung it in a low sweep at both rioters' legs.

Wood cracked against shins and ankles. The rioters cried out as their feet were chopped out from under them. They fell in an ungainly clump of thrashing limbs.

Spotting another opponent, Manning swung sharply about and slashed the two-by-four into the newest threat. The enemy, batted eight feet, crashed into a building and slumped to the sidewalk, stunned.

Captain Takutu opened the driver's door and stepped unsteadily from the bus. He had been physically and emotionally shaken by the collision with the lamp post and the unexpected attack. Takutu shook his head to clear it and reached for the pistol on his hip. Fumbling with the button-flap holster, he glanced up to see several Indian rioters rushing toward him.

"Oh, God!" Takutu gasped, and clawed open the holster.

A well-built Indian jumped the captain and clamped a hand around his wrist, pushing Takutu's gun-hand back against the bus. In his other hand, the rioter held a heavy-bladed hunting knife. Takutu gripped the Indian's forearm and tried to hold the knife at bay, but the rioter was pumped up with fury. The captain was still shaken by the suddenness of the ambush and the bus crash. He was unable to raise the pistol and the Indian steadily moved the blade closer to his throat.

Suddenly the rioter yelped with pain. His fist popped open, and the knife fell from his trembling fingers. A deep gash on the back of his hand bled as the Indian glanced at the source of his agony. Rafael Encizo stood beside the rioter and Captain Takutu. The Cuban held a Cold Steel Tanto fighting knife in his fist. A ribbon of blood stained the six-inch blade.

Encizo thrust his other arm forward and stamped the heel of his palm into the Indian's skull. The man stumbled. Takutu broke free and slapped the barrel of his pistol across the Indian's head. The guy dropped unconscious at Takutu's feet.

Another Indian rioter charged toward Encizo, swinging a rake overhead. The Cuban ducked. The metal teeth of the rake slammed into the roof of the bus. The shaft vibrated less than an inch from Encizo's bowed head. Lunging, the Phoenix commando delivered a cross-body slash with his Tanto. The attacker screamed as the ultrasharp steel sliced his thigh muscle.

Encizo rammed his free fist under the guy's ribs and raised the Cold Steel blade, cutting the Indian's forearm. The rake clattered to the ground as the rioter retreated, limping and cradling his wounded arm. Another rioter had been about to come to the aid of his comrade, but backed off when he saw Encizo's uncanny speed and expertise with a knife.

Katz also emerged from the bus. An Indian opponent attacked the Israeli and lashed out with a fillet knife. Katz raised his prosthesis and blocked the knife stroke. The thin blade bounced off the Phoenix commander's artificial limb. Katz swung the steel hooks of his prosthesis in a short swooping gesture before the startled opponent could react to the surprise of cutting an individual who apparently didn't bleed. The metal claws suddenly clamped around the fillet knife. Katz twisted the prosthesis and snapped the thin blade in two.

"Go home!" Katz ordered as he drew his Walther P-88 pistol with his left hand and pointed it at the Indian's dumbfounded face.

The man turned and ran straight into another rioter. Both men staggered backward, watching Katz's weapon, then ran. The Phoenix Force commander raised his arm high and fired two shots from the Walther autoloader into the sky. The warning startled the other combatants. Indian and black Guyanese alike backed off when they heard the shots and saw orange flames jet from the pistol barrel into the night.

The other members of Phoenix Force took this as a cue and also yanked pistols from shoulder leather. McCarter wielded his Browning Hi-Power, the others Walther P-88 autos. Captain Takutu also held his pistol, but seemed unsure what he should do with it. Colonel Barama climbed from the bus, gun in hand. Sutcliffe remained inside the vehicle. The CIA case officer wasn't armed.

The rioters retreated. Sirens wailed as police cars sped to the scene. Two firetrucks raced up the streets to the burning church and other blazing buildings. The mob seemed to be breaking up, and the angry shouts and threats were gradually replaced by sobs and soft words of comfort. The rioters were no longer fighting each other, but concerned with their personal loss.

"Well, that was an interesting little donnybrook," McCarter commented as he slipped his Browning into the leather harness under his arm. "I wonder what it was all about."

"Maybe we'll find out later," Katz replied. "Right now we have to get out of here and concentrate on our mission. Colonel Barama, we'd like to hear more about what you were saying before this interruption."

"Yes," the colonel said with a nod. "I was suggesting the People's Temple might be responsible for the murders at the village."

"I considered that theory absurd," Sutcliffe said as he stepped unsteadily from the bus. The CIA man glanced at the burning buildings and the remnants of the mob still in the streets. "Now, I'm not so sure. It seems there's some sort of madness spreading through Guyana. The sort of madness that gets people killed."

4

Colonel Barama had set up a safehouse in a warehouse at a lumberyard on the outskirts of Georgetown. The building was crowded with stacks of boards, sheets of plywood and machinery. It was far from an ideal temporary base, but it offered tight security. The safehouse was remote and unoccupied except for two night watchmen employed by Barama. It was an unlikely place for such a meeting, which somehow made it more desirable.

Phoenix Force and Sutcliffe sat on folding chairs in a semicircle at a bay area, surrounded by piles of lumber. A naked bulb cast dim light from the ceiling. Barama unlocked a steel file cabinet, opened a drawer and extracted four folders. He handed them to Katz.

"As I'm sure you can imagine," Barama began as he headed back to the file cabinet, "Guyana was shocked and alarmed by the Jonestown massacre in 1978. The rest of the world was appalled, but the incident had an even greater effect on us because it happened in our country. Some even blamed us for what happened. More than nine hundred ghosts continue to haunt Guyana. A number of strange stories were told after the massacre, horror stories that seemed absurd at the time. Stories about survivors from Jonestown who still lived in the jungles."

"Some people think Elvis is still alive, too," Calvin James remarked. "There are lots of weird stories floatin' around. James Dean, Marilyn Monroe, Bruce Lee and other celebrities were all supposed to have faked their deaths, according to the tabloids. There was even one sick rumor that President Kennedy hadn't been killed by the sniper bullets in Dallas, that he had been reduced to a human vegetable after the shooting. They said he was hidden away at a secret clinic on an island somewhere so the world would never know his terrible fate. Funny how the only reporters who ever 'break' these 'super-secret stories' are writing for the sleaziest trash publications on the stands.''

"That's what most of us thought about the claims about deranged survivors of Jonestown,'' Barama assured him.

"Before we left the States, we discussed the possibility that a branch of the People's Temple might be involved in the most recent tragedy,'' Rafael Encizo reminded the others. "We've seen a lot of incredible things ourselves over the years. I wouldn't be too quick to dismiss any possibility just yet.''

"There are four separate incidents of Guyanese found dead in or near the jungle in the area of the Essequibo River,'' Katz announced as he skimmed over the reports Barama had given him. "The incidents occurred over a three-year period. Each involved two or more people, and all died from cyanide poisoning. Deaths are listed as homicides, but evidence can't confirm whether these were suicide or murder.''

"Exactly,'' the colonel confirmed. "Four incidents of mysterious deaths that occurred before the massacre at the village. We've tried to keep these deaths from becoming public knowledge over the years until we could find out what was really happening. Of course, one can't stop rumors and speculation. We did manage to prevent the stories from becoming an international scandal, but we still haven't learned whether there really is a group of insane survivors of Jim Jones's commune of death running about in the jungle somewhere."

"That does seem pretty hard to believe," Gary Manning said. "Still, a lot of people are definitely dead, and I don't imagine there's a virus in the air that encourages people to commit suicide."

"And conveniently supplies them with cyanide to do it with," McCarter added. The British ace rose from his chair and began to pace. A constant bundle of nervous energy, McCarter could never stay seated for long. "There must be something going on in the rain forest that somebody reckons is worth killing for. I seem to recall there are gold mines here in Guyana. Maybe somebody has been prospecting in the area and they're trying to frighten away others who might get close to the evidence that suggested there was a mother lode out there."

"Every gold mine I have knowledge of in this country has been located in the mountains to the south," Barama replied. "I doubt the killers have found some undiscovered underground fortune."

"A gold mine wouldn't explain why the killers slaughtered the villagers," James added. "That village had been there for nearly a century. Anybody who's been killing off folks for the last three years because they might get too close would have done something to the village before now."

"What about coca plants?" Encizo inquired. "There are very large and ruthless criminal syndicates in South America involved in the cocaine trade. Especially Colombian and Bolivian mobs. Perhaps someone is trying to start a new harvest of coca plants here, as well."

"I doubt that," Barama stated. "I've never known of anyone growing coca plants in Guyana. We don't have a serious drug problem here compared to most other South American countries. Certainly not compared to Mexico or the United States."

"We might have a better idea who we're after if we inspect the village," Manning suggested. "That seemed to be a pretty nasty riot we came upon when we entered the city. Is this sort of thing common in Georgetown or anywhere else in Guyana?"

"You think the riot could be related to the massacre?" Sutcliffe asked, frowning. "I'd say that's grasping for straws, gentlemen."

"So, let us grasp a little," James told him. "In case you failed to notice, that was a race war between blacks and Indians. Do the two ethnic groups usually get along this badly, or did we just happen to arrive at a bad time?"

"There is occasional unrest between blacks and Indians in Guyana," Barama admitted, reluctant to discuss the subject. "We have cultural and traditional differences. There are also religious differences. These are not necessarily divided on ethnic lines. There are Christian blacks and Indians in Guyana, Catholic as well as Protestant. Of course, about half our population aren't Christians. Hindus comprise roughly thirty-four percent of our people. There's also a fairly large Muslim community and other religions with smaller numbers of followers."

"Are most of the clashes between Indians and blacks related to religion?" Manning probed.

"No," Barama replied. "The most serious racial violence in Guyana occurred in the early sixties after the British agreed to allow Guyana full internal self-government. Cheddi Jagan of the People's Progressive

Party became president. His party ran the legislative branch, and Jagan's economic policies were very unpopular with many black Guyanese. Many Indians supported Jagan. Perhaps I should explain: the Indians who supported him were fellow East Indians, persons of the same ethnic descent as myself. Not Indians from North America—I believe you call them Native Americans now.''

"North American Indians?'' James asked with surprise. "You mean like Cherokee, Sioux, Apaches, those sort of Indians?''

"I don't know if we have any Apaches,'' Barama answered, "but Indians from a number of North American tribes immigrated to British Guiana in the nineteenth century. Some of them still retained their tribal languages and customs. Most Guyanese, regardless of racial background, tend to live in communities that are comprised of members of their own ethnic group.''

"You mean segregated,'' James said.

"Not by government action,'' the colonel assured him. "We simply favor our own people in different groups that share a common culture and ethnic origin. You'll see cities and towns that are more integrated, but these are divided into neighborhoods that are predominantly Indian or black.''

"Sort of like ghettos, huh?'' James snorted.

"You won't see much extreme poverty in the cities, and none of it is concentrated in any particular racial group,'' Barama declared. "As I explained, the only serious racial troubles have been caused by one group believing the other has superior political power. It happened when Jagan was president, but there wasn't such trouble when Burnham took office in 1964. He was a black man, you know.''

"Well, something sure had those blokes stirred up this evening," McCarter commented. "They were half-crazy with rage and terror."

Captain Takutu rose from a stool by a field radio in a corner. He removed a headset and spoke into the microphone before ending transmission. The captain joined the others.

"I spoke with the Georgetown Police," Takutu announced. "They say the riot was started when a group of Indians deliberately set fire to the church. Supposedly these same vandals also attacked some black civilians on the street. Details are still cloudy, but that's how it looks so far."

"Any suspicions why this happened now?" Sutcliffe inquired.

"Not yet," the captain answered. "But there was a similar incident in New Amsterdam tonight. Allegedly a group of blacks broke into a mosque during evening prayers. They hurled torches at the Indian Muslims and threw a copy of the Koran to the ground and trampled it. As if that wasn't enough to offend the Muslims, one of the vandals apparently dropped a copy of *The Satanic Verses* when he fled the scene."

"Salman Rushdie's book? The one that stirred up such a fuss with the Islamic community in general and the Ayatollah in particular? Now, who would do that?" Manning shook his head. "This sounds like a definite setup."

"The riots may not be connected with our mission," Katz said thoughtfully. The Israeli fired up a Camel cigarette and blew smoke through his nostrils. Then he added, "One thing in our favor is that the riots will attract the attention of most of the reporters who came to cover the story about the cyanide deaths and the disappearance of Bob Handel and his girlfriend. That should give us a better opportunity to check the crime scene first thing in the morning."

"Why wait until morning?" Sutcliffe inquired. "Why not do it now?"

"Because we can't look for clues in the dark," Manning informed him. "We'd have to use floodlights, infrared, hand-held flashlights and other special gear. All that new activity and lights at the village would be bound to attract the media, and they'd be back in droves."

"Drawn by a thousand points of light," James remarked with a wiry grin.

"Cute," Manning said with a weary nod. "Besides, trying to find clues at night is nearly impossible, even with the artificial lights and special gear. Oh, if we had arrived within a couple hours after the incident, we'd use heat detectors that would have picked up the recent footprints, maybe even have tracked the people responsible. But we didn't get here soon enough. So we'll have to wait a few hours and do the job right without attracting a lot of attention."

"You really think you'll find anything the Guyanese investigation overlooked?" Sutcliffe asked pessimistically.

"It's a place to start," Katz told the CIA man. "So far you haven't been very helpful. I realize you're not accustomed to missions of this sort. I'm trying to remind myself over and over again that you've spent most of your career with the Company behind a desk, and your assignment in Guyana has been a simple and safe liaison Intelligence position at the American Embassy."

"So I'm not a brawler or a gunfighter," Sutcliffe said, sniffling. "I admit that. That's not what Intelligence work is about. Maybe the President enlisted you five from the O.K. Corral, but my job has consisted of gathering information and evaluating it for the good of the United States of America. It may not be showy or openly heroic, but it's necessary for the sake of national security.''

''I'm not questioning your courage or the importance of your job,'' Katz assured him. The Israeli stuck his cigarette butt in an empty beer can and heard it sizzle in the dregs of liquid inside. ''You're not armed and you're obviously not trained in hand-to-hand combat, so the best thing you could have done when we clashed with the mob this evening was to stay in the bus and let us handle the situation.''

''I am armed and I am trained in hand-to-hand,'' Colonel Barama remarked, ''but I wasn't much help. You gentlemen didn't seem to need any. I must admit, I was impressed by your... agility.''

''So was I,'' Captain Takutu admitted. ''Taking on multiple armed opponents without killing or seriously injuring any of them is quite a feat.''

''The rioters weren't trained fighters,'' Encizo said. ''They weren't really familiar with violence, either. They were just a group of people who snapped when violence erupted around them. For every person running around in a frenzy in the street, there were probably twenty who didn't respond that way.''

''What a generous evaluation,'' Sutcliffe commented. He sounded bored and annoyed by the conversation. ''You guys are even giving me a chance to save face. No need for that. I do my job. That doesn't include playing commando games.''

''This is no game,'' Katz told him in a hard voice. ''You've done little more than whine since you met us.''

"There hasn't been much for me to do so far," the CIA man said defensively.

"You can contact Company Intelligence sources in Guyana and neighboring South American countries to see if anyone knows anything that might help," Encizo said. "Is there an escalation of cocaine syndicate operations in this region of South America? Have people been poisoned in other countries, or have rumors about the People's Temple surfaced recently in Brazil or Venezuela?"

"All right," Sutcliffe replied. "I'll see to that. It's probably a waste of time, but I won't argue with you. I figure you fellows probably have the same theory about this business I have. All these other notions are just covering all the bases. Those people were all killed Jim Jones-style to distract us from the real reason it was done."

"So, you have it figured out?" McCarter said dryly. "Share this great knowledge with the rest of us."

"It's obvious," Sutcliffe declared. "Whoever did it kidnapped the Handel boy and probably his girlfriend, as well. They're holding them somewhere—probably in a city, not in the jungle—and they'll make ransom demands in a day or two. They may have already contacted the senator."

"You might be right," Gary Manning said. "There have been a lot of kidnappings in Italy by criminal gangs, and many terrorist acts have been committed for financial rather than political gain. Still, that doesn't change the fact we start looking for these bastards pretty much the same way until we know more about what we're up against."

"I'd like to examine some of the bodies myself," James told the two Guyanese officers. "I might catch something your medical examiners overlooked. I've done a lot of autopsies on homicide victims over the years, including some that were pretty unusual—even a few poison victims."

"You're a doctor?" Colonel Bárama asked with surprise.

"I don't have enough degrees and certificates to make that claim," James admitted, "but I've had a fair amount of medical training and advanced chemistry. I've had a lot of battlefield experience with treating wounded men, and for the last few years, I've been handling a lot of related matters that include autopsies."

"We can arrange that," Barama assured him. "Do you want to do that tonight or in the morning?"

"As soon as possible," James replied. "Chemical traces in the digestive system, bruises, things like that become harder to evaluate as time passes. I'd better examine the corpses tonight. The rest of you guys might as well get a decent night's sleep before we head out to the village in the morning."

"I've booked reservations for all five of you at the Royal Inn," Sutcliffe declared. "It's one of the best hotels in Guyana. The restaurant is very good. Seafood is excellent here."

"All right," Katz said with a nod. "We'd better arrive at the hotel separately. Someone may have described us from the fight with the rioters this evening. If all five of us show up at once, it might raise a few eyebrows and make some people suspicious. The Soviet KGB certainly has people in Georgetown. Probably just a listening post, but you never know for sure with Russian Intelligence. We've clashed with the KGB on quite a few missions in the past. They've certainly got descriptions of us, even if they don't have definite identities for all of us."

"*Glasnost* doesn't change your attitude about the Russians?" Captain Takutu inquired.

"I don't have anything against the Russian people," Katz assured him. "But I certainly don't trust the KGB, and I'm not convinced the changes in the Soviet government will prove to be permanent. I hope the *glasnost* policies are genuine reforms and the Soviet Union will change for the better. Yet I still have to remain skeptical even if I'd like to be optimistic. Trust isn't part of our business. We have to remain suspicious of the motives of our allies, let alone nations of the Communist bloc."

"Do you think the KGB is responsible for what happened in the village?" Sutcliffe asked.

"I'm not ruling out anything just yet," the Phoenix commander stated. "But I'd say this doesn't sound like a KGB operation. We have to maintain security precautions anyway. Turner and Carver can go on to the hotel first."

"Lucky us," McCarter muttered. Carver was his cover name for the mission, and Turner was Manning's current alias. "That ought to be bloody boring."

"Considering how often people are trying to kill us," Manning commented dryly, "I don't mind being bored once in a while."

5

The desk clerk at the Royal Inn checked the registration list, found Manning's and McCarter's pseudonyms and handed them the keys to their rooms. Did they need a hand with their luggage? The Phoenix Force pair, having left their rifle cases at the safehouse, carried only two aluminum suitcases and their briefcases.

"Could you lock up our luggage?" Manning inquired as he signed the register. "We've heard you have a fine restaurant and we'd like to have dinner." The desk clerk took their bags into a back room, but McCarter and Manning held on to their attaché cases. Manning handed the clerk five Guyanese dollars, roughly equivalent to American currency but with a far greater purchasing power.

The Phoenix commandos crossed the lobby to the restaurant, where the maître d'hôtel greeted them and escorted them to a table. There were plenty of tables to choose from; only two were occupied. At one table sat two Indians, quietly drinking tea and whispering back and forth as if they were in a library. The other party consisted of five people—white, well dressed, and apparently upper-middle-class.

Wealthy tourists? Manning glanced at the group. The guy at the head of the table sat erect, shoulders squared and head held high. He wore a white dinner jacket and black bow tie. To his left was a younger man in his late teens, slender with frail features that seemed almost sickly by candlelight. A woman across from the young guy appeared to be in her late thirties or early forties. Her white dress seemed almost Victorian with its high lacy collar and long sleeves. She wore her blond hair braided and wound around her head like a halo.

The two others at the table didn't seem accustomed to formal evening clothes. They were big, heavily muscled men who would have looked perfectly at home on a gridiron with football helmets on their heavy skulls. The pair watched the Phoenix Force pros as if they thought Manning and McCarter would rob the place. Bodyguards, Manning thought. Either that, or they were the toughest and most suspicious-looking pair of accountants the Canadian had ever seen.

Otto Weissflog noticed the Phoenix commandos but didn't stare as Werner and Reinhard were doing. The Nazi glanced over his shoulder and saw Manning and McCarter were about to sit at another table. He raised a hand and waved at the maître d'.

"I'd like to invite the gentlemen to join us at my table," he said. "Put their dinner on my bill."

McCarter looked at Manning and raised his eyebrows. The Canadian shrugged in reply. The invitation seemed friendly enough. Perhaps too friendly. Manning realized he tended to be a bit paranoid after being with Phoenix Force for so many years. Still, they were looking for information about recent events in Guyana, and one never knows from what source Intelligence might arrive.

"That's a very generous offer," the Canadian told Weissflog.

"Let's take him up on it," McCarter told Manning.

Manning grunted. The guy at the table spoke with a British accent. Manning didn't relish the idea of sitting down to eat with McCarter and his new-found buddy chatting about the British economy and how many times Big Ben had malfunctioned in the past twenty years. He knew McCarter had not been back to his homeland for almost a year, and the British ace would probably enjoy talking to a fellow countryman about England.

"Okay," the Canadian agreed. He figured he could risk being bored for an hour or two.

The two muscle boys moved extra chairs to the table to accommodate the Phoenix pair. A waiter set places for the new guests. Weissflog smiled broadly and nodded with pleasure when the strangers accepted his invitation. Karin Weissflog's lips curled in imitation of a smile as she glanced nervously at the pair. The bodyguards did not seem happy that strangers had joined them and continued to watch Manning and Carter as if they were outpatients from a lunatic asylum.

"I'm glad you decided to join us," Weissflog declared. "I rarely have the opportunity to talk with visitors from America or Great Britain. I'm Stanley Wilkens. This is my wife, Carol, and my son, John."

He tilted his head toward the pasty-faced youth.

"My associates are Mr. Beatrix and Mr. Aschwin," Weissflog added, gesturing toward the bodyguards. "They're my personal security, you might say. What with terrorism and criminal organizations being what they are these days, no one can be too careful. Even here in Guyana. I understand there was a riot in the city earlier this evening."

"We were lucky enough to arrive in Georgetown after it was over," Manning said. He introduced himself as Eric Turner and McCarter as Daniel Carver.

"I'm very pleased to meet you," Weissflog assured them. "You're Americans?"

"No, I'm British and Turner is Canadian," McCarter replied. "We're journalists for an international publication called *Commonwealth Today*. We handle stories about events going on in member nations of the Commonwealth."

"That includes Guyana, of course," Weissflog remarked. "So, what stories are you covering here? That dreadful business with the mass suicide, I suppose."

"It's news, Mr. Wilkens," Manning stated. "You're a native Guyanese?"

"Oh, yes," Weissflog answered. "Of British descent, of course. Mr. Aschwin and Mr. Beatrix are from the Netherlands Antilles. Beautiful Caribbean islands. Have you ever been there?"

"Not yet," McCarter admitted.

The waiter came to take their orders. Weissflog suggested the lobster. They took his advice. Both commandos politely passed on the white wine Weissflog's party drank with their meal. Manning ordered coffee and McCarter asked if they had Coca Cola.

"Coke Classic, if you have it," the Briton added.

"I'll check with the kitchen, sir."

Weissflog frowned, disappointed that a Briton would order an American soft drink with a meal that obviously demanded a fine imported white wine. He didn't realize McCarter had developed a fondness for Coca Cola after spending years as an SAS soldier in Oman and a special observer in Vietnam. The combination of extreme hot weather and the fact that water was either unsafe due to bacteria or deliberate sabotage by the enemy had made him appreciate a nice cold bottle of Coke with the metal cap firmly stamped down before he popped it open.

"How long has your family lived in Guyana?" Manning asked their host as the waiter placed a cup of coffee by his plate.

"My father moved here in the late 1930s," Weissflog replied. "He bought the plantation that I still run to this day. Sugarcane. We've been blessed with considerable success over the years. Still, it can be difficult being a member of a minority group here. White Lutherans are as rare as hens' teeth here."

"What's your opinion of the alleged suicide at the village?" the Canadian inquired.

"I really don't have one," Weissflog said, shrugging. "I've heard rumors about the People's Temple still being active in the jungles ever since that tragedy in 1978. Never thought too much of it one way or the other. I haven't seen any proof that any of those stories are true."

"Please," Karin began in a quiet voice as she looked down at her plate. "May we change the subject?"

"Of course, Mrs. Wilkens," Manning replied. "It's hardly a fit topic for the dinner table. I apologize and can only say that we journalists tend to get a bit obsessive when we're pursuing a story. Sometimes we forget our manners."

"That was pretty bloody careless of you, Turner," McCarter muttered.

Manning was tempted to kick McCarter under the table, but he was afraid he might boot the wrong person's shin.

"I've never been to London," Gerhart Weissflog began. The youth directed his comment to McCarter. "What's it like, Mr. Carver?"

"That rather depends on what part of the city you're talking about," McCarter replied. "Westminster Abbey is a bit solemn, but certainly interesting. Monuments, tombs, cathedrals and Gothic buildings. Joseph Addison once said it was a place for taking a walk when 'in a serious humor.' But you certainly wouldn't describe Chelsea or Piccadilly that way.''

Weissflog mentioned that Hyde Park was one of his favorite spots in London and asked McCarter whether it was still a charming and quaint place to spend an afternoon. Manning nearly scoffed. Imagine asking McCarter to evaluate how ''quaint'' anything is, the Canadian thought. The Briton avoided the question by saying he hadn't been to Hyde Park for a long time and his job usually had him traveling far from London. That much was certainly true.

Manning was glad their food arrived as McCarter and the Wilkens family continued to talk about England. He thought the two bodyguards also felt left out of the conversation and asked how they wound up moving from the Netherlands Antilles to Guyana.

''Why do you ask?'' Reinhard replied suspiciously, his English thickly accented. His *W* sounded like an English *V* and his *T*s resembled *D*s.

''He is a journalist, Aschwin,'' Werner told his companion. ''They are always curious. How we came to Guyana is a long and dull story, Mr. Turner. We used to be policemen in the Antilles. Did not pay very good. We make more money as Mr. Wilkens's security.''

''I see,'' Manning replied, sorry he asked. Their accent was familiar to him, and it didn't sound Dutch.

The conversation remained pleasant, if formal. Weissflog dominated it with stories about his infrequent trips to England and the sugarcane trade. His son asked several questions about Britain and a few about Canada, which allowed Manning to occasionally join the discussion. Even Karin had a few remarks about shopping on Oxford and Bond streets when she accompanied her husband on a visit to London.

"And isn't Fleet Street dreadful?" she added. "Those trashy rubbish publications they peddle ought to be outlawed. Don't you agree?"

"I wouldn't say they should be outlawed," McCarter answered, "but I think they ought to get sued more often for some of the things they print."

"That sort of thing wouldn't have been tolerated in the England my father told me about," Weissflog declared. He shook his head sadly. "What's become of morality? Not just in England, mind you. Look at what a cesspool the United States has become. Homosexuals march in the streets and demand equal rights, as if perverts should be allowed any rights, period. Communists run for political office, and private citizens are allowed to own firearms. No wonder their government can't control their people. Especially—" he checked to make certain the black Guyanese waiter was beyond earshot "—all those Negroes and Orientals and God knows what else. No decent farmer would let his cattle crossbreed the way different races do in America. Of course, you've got the same problem in England and Canada. No standards for the population. No controls."

"Well, I guess you have a right to your opinion," Manning said, trying to keep from revealing the contempt he felt for Wilkens's statements. "Thank you for dinner, but we have to be going now."

"Oh," Weissflog said with a frown, clearly disappointed. "Are you sure? I thought we might have some brandy and cigars."

"We don't—" McCarter began, an edge in his voice and anger in his eyes, but he managed to restrain himself and speak in a calm voice as he continued "—have the luxury of stayin' up much later. Busy day tomorrow, you know. Back to work, nose to the grindstone, all that rot."

"I understand," Weissflog assured them. "It's been a pleasure meeting you both. I hope we come across each other again."

"That's possible," Manning replied.

Neither Phoenix commando wanted to shake hands with Weissflog, so they stepped away from the tables and nodded their farewells. They walked from the dining room and waved the waiter to come to them. He obliged.

"Yes, gentlemen?" the waiter inquired. "Is something wrong?"

"We're paying our own tab tonight," Manning said, handing the waiter forty Guyanese dollars. "Does that cover it?"

"Almost," the waiter said. "It's forty-five, total, for both of you. Mr. Wilkens fully intended to pay."

"We don't want his generosity, and if he's offended that's bloody tough shit," McCarter declared as he handed the waiter another twenty. "That'll cover the meals and your tip. You sure as hell won't get a decent tip from that stuffy bastard."

"I never have in the past," the waiter commented with a sly grin. "Thank you both and have a pleasant evening."

They entered the lobby to discover Yakov Katzenelenbogen and Rafael Encizo at the front desk. The pair signed the register as their partners approached.

"You guys eat yet?" Manning inquired. "The food here's pretty good, but the company might be lousy after a while."

"We already ate," Katz assured him. The Israeli glanced from Manning to McCarter. "You two look as if something rubbed you the wrong way."

"Pretty rare that the same thing would annoy you both equally," Encizo added, well aware the Canadian and Briton had very different personalities.

"Just had dinner with a chap who seemed to be a decent sort except he was a bit windy and full of himself," McCarter replied. "Toward the end he started to come up with stuff we didn't care to listen to. Not worth talkin' about, really."

"Yeah," Manning agreed. He turned to the desk clerk. "May we get out bags now?"

The man behind the desk retrieved their aluminum suitcases. The four Phoenix pros mounted the stairs with their baggage in hand. On the second floor they searched for their rooms. Katz found his first and put his suitcase down in order to use the key in his left hand. The hooks of his prosthesis held the handle to his valise.

"I take it you two had dinner with a bigot of some sort," he remarked, and glanced at Manning and McCarter.

"How'd you guess?" the Canadian inquired.

"Our little group is certainly interracial," Katz said with a smile. "You can't work with four men and become as close to them as if they were your brothers and still have much tolerance for someone trashing their ethnic group. I don't even like the word 'goy' any more. It doesn't mean anything other than referring to someone as 'not a Jew,' but I've heard too many people use it in a contemptuous and arrogant manner to be comfortable with that expression now."

"Well, we'd hoped we might hear some local opinion about the so-called mass suicide," McCarter said. "But

Wilkens didn't have anything to add to what we already know.''

"Forget about him," Encizo advised. "We've got a job to concentrate on. Cal is at the morgue, examining dead bodies."

"Some guys get all the luck," Manning said dryly.

"He'll meet us tomorrow morning," Katz declared. "Get some sleep, because we've got a long day ahead of us."

6

The village did not look like the scene of mass destruction. The bodies had been removed, and the press had lost interest in the actual site of the disaster. The dirt streets and crudely made houses were quiet and abandoned. Even the domesticated animals were gone. The village was empty. It could have been a housing project for peasants, yet to be occupied.

Only four soldiers guarded the village as Phoenix Force, Colonel Barama and Captain Takutu arrived early one morning. They parked their Land Rovers near an army truck, emerged from the vehicles and approached an NCO on guard duty. The sergeant snapped his heels together and saluted. The officers returned the gesture.

"At ease, soldier," Barama told him. "Report what's happened during your time on watch."

"Not much, sir," the sergeant replied. "Most of the newspaper and television reporters left before we arrived. They were more interested in covering the riots last night. The few that remained left soon after we started our watch. Since it was so quiet, the rest of our unit was called back to base in case the forces dealing with the riots needed reinforcements. I was put in charge of guard duty here. No one has been here until you arrived, Colonel."

"Very good," Barama said. He turned toward Phoenix Force. "Help yourselves, gentlemen. I hope you find something we missed."

Gary Manning examined the ground by some old tire tracks. The Canadian frowned. Despite the military's efforts to keep the press at bay, there were dozens of footprints stamped over one another and across the tire tracks. Many might have belonged to those who removed the corpses from the site. It was impossible to tell from such a mess. The Canadian knelt, moving from one spot to another in a vain effort to find some useful clue.

"The Guyanese trackers that examined the trail earlier came up with more than I can now," Manning confessed. "Maybe I can find something in the fields."

Rafael Encizo headed for the houses and entered one. He found no signs of a struggle there, nor in any of the other dwellings. However, he noticed that there were no locks or bolts on any of the doors. A peaceful, crime-free society had no need for such contrivances. The villagers had had nothing worth stealing. Katz appeared at the doorway as Encizo inspected the last house.

"Find anything?" the Cuban inquired.

"You, Cal and Gary are more experienced with criminal investigations than I am," the Phoenix commander admitted. "I've been doing little more than checking the books and newspapers in the village to see if anyone here was interested in radical politics, the People's Temple or anything else out of the ordinary that might explain why this happened. I found some elementary schoolbooks printed in English and some old newspapers and magazines also in English. Most of the publications here are in Hindi. Maybe Barama can translate them, but I doubt any of this stuff is subversive."

"Well, I haven't found anything," Encizo confessed. "No traces of ether or kerosene to suggest they might have been involved in processing cocaine. No weapons, hardly any money in the whole village. The fact there's any at all means robbery wasn't the motive, unless whoever wasted these people was smart enough to leave a few Guyanese dollars and some coins. But I really don't think the villagers were sitting on a secret fortune."

"Neither do I," Katz agreed as he glanced about the simple two-room dwelling. There were blankets on the floor, a tiny wood-burning stove, a low table with candles and a tiny clay statue of Lord Sri Krishna, the Hindu supreme personality of the Godhead. "If the villagers were gangsters or terrorists, I'd be very surprised."

"I can't imagine it, either," Encizo agreed. "But I can't see any reason anyone would have to kill them. I don't believe the mass suicide theory."

Outside, Calvin James was examining an alley between two houses. The black commando dug up some loose soil with the blade of his Blackmoor Dirk. Then he pushed the dirt back into the hole.

"Looked like something had been buried there recently," he explained, sliding the knife into the scabbard under his right arm. "Just some seeds."

"You didn't find anything, either?" Encizo asked.

"Nope," James admitted. "Didn't really think I would, either. Seems pretty obvious somebody just rounded up the villagers and made 'em drink poisoned fruit juice. They were pacifists, so they didn't resist. Probably wouldn't have done them any good if they tried."

"So, what was the motive?" Encizo asked.

"I don't know," James admitted. "But I find it pretty hard to believe a bunch of crazy survivors of the Jonestown massacre are hiding out in the jungles and occasionally swooping down on victims and making them guzzle poison punch. For one thing, I don't think there would be enough wackos left over from the Jim Jones incident to pull off something like this. The People's Temple didn't teach followers how to live off the land in a goddamn tropical rain forest. I'm also wondering how these dudes came up with enough cyanide and how they coerced people to drink the stuff."

"Guards at Jonestown were armed with assault rifles," Encizo reminded him.

"You figure the survivors also took enough ammunition to last twelve years?" James said, shaking his head. "I don't know who did it, but I bet it wasn't any of Jim Jones's leftovers."

"They wanted us to believe this was the work of People's Temple fanatics," Katz stated. "Which leaves us with the twin questions of who did it and why. The villagers don't seem to be a logical target. Maybe the real target was the American team headed by the Handel lad. He's missing, so there's a chance he and his girlfriend are still alive."

"Sounds like you're leaning toward Sutcliffe's theory," Encizo commented.

"He might be right," Katz replied. "The biggest problem I have with that theory is it doesn't explain why all these people were killed. Kidnappers could have abducted Bob Handel before he reached the village or after he left. Why kill all these villagers when it would have been easier and more practical simply to ambush Bob's group at a more remote spot?"

"Shit," James muttered. "Instead of getting closer to answers, we're just turning up more questions."

The three Phoenix pros headed back to the Land Rovers. Barama waited for them while Takutu sat in a vehicle and reported their arrival to Georgetown. Manning continued to search the crop fields for some evidence while McCarter wandered into the jungle. Encizo, seeing the Briton slip into the foliage, clucked his tongue.

"What does that loco London-bred Englishman think he's doing out there?" the Cuban wondered aloud.

"Probably just takin' a leak," James said with a shrug.

Katz handed some books in Hindi to Barama. The colonel looked at the cover of the first one and grunted.

"It's the *Bhagavad Gita*," he explained. "The main text of Vedic philosophy. Hindu scriptures, you might say."

"I saw several copies of this book in the village," Katz explained. "I thought it was probably a religious book."

"The other books are poetry—based on Hindu beliefs, no doubt—a biography of Gandhi and a history book." Barama opened the last book and checked the copyright page. "It was printed in 1958. The villagers were not terribly concerned with current events."

"Maybe not," James commented, "but they became a current news item anyway."

Manning shuffled between the corn stalks and approached the others. The Canadian didn't appear to have any more success than his fellow Phoenix members, but he tended to wear a poker face under most circumstances.

"I found a set of tire tracks that extend to the village and seem to originate back in the thicket," Manning announced. "They haven't been ruined, so maybe we can track them back to the jungle. That's going to take a lot of time, fellas."

"What do you mean by a lot?" James asked. "Hours or days?"

"Hours," the Canadian replied. "If we're lucky."

"Hey, you blokes!" McCarter shouted from the jungle. "I found something!"

The other four Phoenix Force commandos were surprised by the Briton's call. James and Manning jogged toward the rain forest as McCarter emerged, holding a penlike object. Sunlight reflected on the brass cartridge casing.

"I'll be damned," Manning remarked as he drew closer. "How'd you manage this?"

"While you were mucking about in the fields," the Briton answered. "I just strolled in the opposite direction. Found some pretty obvious horse hoofprints and followed them to the bush. Found bloodstains on some ferns and looked around some more. That's when I spotted this shell casing."

"What caliber?" James inquired as he caught up with Manning.

"Nine millimeter parabellum," McCarter replied, and handed the casing to Manning. "Notice the stamp on the rim around the primer."

"IMBEL," Manning read the legend aloud. The letters formed a tiny horseshoe pattern along the rim of the shell casing. The primer in the center had been punctured by a firing pin.

"Is that supposed to mean something?" James asked.

"IMBEL is the national arms manufacturing outfit in Brazil," Manning explained. "The government runs it. This cartridge was military issue in Brazil. The brass isn't stripped, and the crimp fanned out pretty evenly."

"Subguns tend to batter brass quite a bit," McCarter added. "I reckon it was fired by a pistol and a well-made one. Primer was hit dead-center by the firing pin. The crimp also suggests it was probably 115-grain NATO hardball ammo. No hot loads. Either strict military ammo or reloaded by the book.''

"That's a lot of assumptions," Manning said with a shrug. "But I wouldn't be surprised if you're right. Let's see if we can find anything else."

"Let me bag that shell casing," James said, taking a small clear plastic bag from a pocket. "Maybe we'll get lucky and there'll be a fingerprint or two on the brass."

They spent more than two hours searching the rain forest for more evidence. Encizo discovered some dried blood on the leaves of a greenheart tree. They didn't know whether the blood was human or animal, but Manning and James agreed the stains appeared to be less than seventy-two hours old, which fit the time of the village massacre.

The Phoenix team moved farther into the jungle. A shape darted along the ground in front of them. Glimpsing a blur of tawny fur, they followed the figure as it ran to the trunk of a tree. The animal scrambled up the tree rapidly, claws grasping bark as its tail swung like a gallows noose. They got a clear view of the creature and saw the large black spots across its yellow fur. Slightly larger than a house cat, it was too small to be a jaguar...unless it was a cub, which meant the mother would be near. A protective mother can be fearsome—especially a jaguar. The largest of the big cats in the western hemisphere, the jaguar is fast and powerful. The mighty cats have been known to break a boar's neck with a single blow and bite through the hide of a crocodile. The four commandos were armed with 9 mm pistols, but no one in his right mind would choose this caliber to try to bring down a jaguar.

"It's an ocelot," Encizo said with a sigh of relief when he saw the cat stare down from the branches of the tree.

The jaguar's smaller cousin watched them approach, hissed and climbed higher. Its natural camouflage soon allowed it to blend into the foliage. The Phoenix warriors moved toward the area where they first saw the cat. Ocelots, like all cats, are carnivorous—meat eaters. They are hunters by nature, but scavengers, as well. It was possible the ocelot was in the area because it smelled blood.

"I got a feeling we're gonna wish we hadn't found this," James commented as they approached a mound of dirt with claw marks where the ocelot had tried to dig to whatever lay buried.

A number of rocks and branches had been placed over the mound in an effort to conceal it. Manning carried a paratrooper's three-fold shovel in a cotton duck-liner attached to his belt. He opened the carrier and removed the shovel. The metal handle snapped into position, and he pushed the steel blade down. The Canadian grimly tightened the lug above the blade. Unfolded, the shovel was twenty-three inches long.

"I don't suppose anyone else thought to bring one of these things along," Manning muttered as he jammed the short spade into the mound.

"We'll have to improvise," McCarter stated, searching for a branch that would serve for a digging tool.

The chore did not take long. Beneath the packed dirt was a shallow grave with two corpses, one male and one female. Dried blood matted the hair of both bodies. James knelt by the corpses and examined them. All four men held their breath as much as possible. The bodies had been buried for less than three days, but the humid weather and burrowing ants had caused enough of a mess to make the dead flesh stink.

"Both Caucasians," James announced as he backed away from the grave and sucked in some fresh air. "Both young, under twenty-four years of age. The guy's head was split open. Looks like a machete or maybe even a sword. Girl was shot in the back of the head. Exit wound blasted an eye out of its socket."

"Jesus," Manning rasped, turning away from the open grave. "Looks like we found Bob Handel and Lynn Carlston."

"Yeah," James agreed with a nod. "So much for Sutcliffe's kidnapping theory."

"No more question about whether the villagers were killed or committed suicide," Encizo added, his voice as hard as iron. "This is definitely murder."

7

"I sent the photo-telex of the dead kids and their fingerprints to the FBI," Sutcliffe began as he took a seat on a crate in the safehouse. "They replied with positive ID on both subjects. It's official—the corpses are Bob Handel and Lynn Carlston."

Phoenix Force and the Guyanese officers were not surprised. They had assembled at the warehouse base outside of Georgetown after returning from the village. Calvin James had supervised autopsies of the murder victims, and Gary Manning had assisted in ballistics at the police headquarters. Both had returned to the safehouse moments before Sutcliffe arrived.

"Has the senator been told?" Rafael Encizo inquired, realizing Sutcliffe probably wouldn't know.

"The Bureau is going to inform the President," the CIA man replied. "I assume he'll tell Senator Handel. I sure don't envy him that task."

"It's very hard to tell someone they lost a loved one," Katz commented in a quiet voice. "It's even harder to be a parent who has lost a son or daughter."

The Israeli spoke from experience. The explosion that cost Katz his right arm during a battle of the Six Day War also killed his only son.

"Anything of interest from ballistics?" Sutcliffe asked.

"The Carlston girl was killed by a nine millimeter bullet," Manning answered. "One hundred and fifteen grain, copper-jacketed hardball slug. The groove marks on the bullet suggest the murder weapon was a late 1930s model Walther P-38, German military manufacture, probably produced by Walther or Spree Werke factories."

"It was a World War II Nazi pistol?" asked the CIA case officer, startled by this claim.

"That's what we suspect, although it isn't definite," the Canadian pro explained as he helped himself to a cup of coffee. "The ammunition is Brazilian, but I understand Guyana doesn't purchase much military hardware or ammo from Brazil."

"Our biggest trade partners are the United Kingdom, Trinidad, Venezuela and the United States," Colonel Barama confirmed. "Most likely the ammunition used by the killer was purchased through black market sources with branches in Brazil."

"So our enemies are probably well armed with illegal gunrunner connections," David McCarter began thoughtfully, taking out a pack of Player's cigarettes. "They have vehicles as well as horses, so there are several of them, if not more than a dozen on up, and they want us to believe People's Temple renegades are responsible for their crimes. The only bodies they tried to hide were the two kids. At least one is armed with a World War II German pistol. That's about all we know."

"No living witnesses to the massacre at the village," Calvin James mused. "Let's try a different tactic. Pretty routine police investigation stuff. Let's question people who live in other villages in the immediate area of the slaughter and ask them if they've noticed anything unusual. We might also try to find anyone who used to live at the village, but moved out recently. Folks in small communities sometimes leave for the big city. To the farmers at that little hamlet, just about any town would seem like goin' off to New York or L.A. Might turn up something.''

"Worth a try," Katz agreed. He took his watch from his shirt pocket. "Good God, it's almost 6 p.m. This has been a long and frustrating day, although we have learned a few things about who we're after."

"Unfortunately not enough to know who they are," Barama said dryly. "I don't know how much manpower the Defense Forces can provide. These outbreaks of riots in my country demand the military concentrate on maintaining order. Both the president of Guyana and the prime minister are being pressured to take action. There's even talk about an emergency meeting of the National Assembly to discuss the possibility of declaring martial law nationwide."

"The riots are that serious?" Encizo asked with surprise. "All this has just sprung up virtually overnight? There was no evidence before the riots started of brewing tensions between racial and religious groups?"

"None whatsoever," Barama responded. "I've never seen anything like this. No one can even tell how it started. Black Christians attacking Indian Hindus and vice versa. Muslims, Christians and Hindus all suddenly at each other's throats. All triggered by seemingly unjustified acts of violence and vandalism. There have even been attacks on some of the North American Indian communities and the handful of Chinese Buddhists in Guyana. The only ethnic group that doesn't seem to be involved are the whites of European descent—which is a very small minority group here."

"Yeah," Manning muttered. "Carver and I met a few of them last night at the restaurant. Hopefully Wilkens isn't a prime example of what they're all like."

"Wilkens?" Barama said with a frown. "He runs a sugar plantation, doesn't he? I've never heard much else about him one way or the other."

"I don't think you want to meet him," McCarter stated. "I'd just as soon we hadn't."

"We realize the riots present an immediate priority for your government and military," Katz told the colonel. "Our mission is important, too, and I'm sure you'll do what you can to help us."

"You have my word on that," Barama assured him.

THE DESK CLERK AT the Royal Inn cheerfully greeted Mr. Turner when Gary Manning entered the hotel lobby. Manning nodded in reply as he headed for the stairs. The Phoneix commando still wore a bush shirt, fatigue trousers and boots. A Minolta camera hung from his neck and he carried his Walther P-88 pistol and shoulder holster rig in a briefcase. Manning galloped upstairs to the second story and headed through the hall to his room.

The Canadian was eager to take a hot bath and change his clothes before dinner. The day's work had been hard and very unpleasant. He wanted to get away from it for an hour or two, but images of two murdered youths plagued his thoughts. Something else also bothered him. A vague suspicion nagged at him from the rim of his subconscious. Manning felt that he had encountered some subtle bit of vital evidence, but he hadn't fully recognized its importance or known what the hell it was. Maybe if he relaxed for a while, the meaning would become clear.

Manning inserted the key in the lock. Entering the room, the Canadian was startled to discover a large black man by the bed. The intruder had pushed back the mattress, and the dresser drawers had been dumped on the floor.

The man glared at Manning, eyes wide and mouth contorted with anger. He was big, but out of shape. The guy's belly bulged over his belt. A large double-edged knife was in his pudgy fist.

Manning wanted to escape into the hall to get some distance between himself and the fat knife artist. If he could buy a couple of seconds, the Canadian could open his valise and draw his pistol. That would tip the scales of the confrontation in his favor. But the door slammed into Manning before he could make a retreat. Another man had been hiding behind the door. The unexpected blow knocked Manning staggering into a wall.

The second opponent slammed the door. A small, wiry black man with a goatlike beard and mustache, he also held a knife. His eyes were wild, like those of a drug addict staring into the realm of a chemical-induced hallucination. His blade jutted from the bottom of his fist in an icepick grip as he charged, knife hand raised for attack.

The Canadian swung his valise. The edge of the briefcase smashed into the skinny attacker's wrist and chopped the knife from the man's hand. Manning shoved an end of the valise into his opponent's face. The blow sent the man reeling, blood oozing from a split lip.

The fat man bellowed and lunged, his knife aimed at the Canadian's stomach. The Phoenix commando used his briefcase as a shield. The blade punched the aluminum valise, and metal snapped on impact. The tip of the blade broke off, only denting the case.

Manning lashed a fist into his opponent's face and drove the corner of his valise into the guy's flabby belly. The fat man stumbled backward, stunned, as his skinny comrade launched another attack. Manning glimpsed motion out of the corner of his eye and turned to see the second opponent leap forward, both hands aimed at the Canadian's neck.

The Phoenix pro swung a forearm high in a rising block and slammed it under the attacker's wrists. The scrawny opponent kicked the valise from Manning's other hand. The Canadian retaliated with a knee to the guy's narrow abdomen and drove his fist under the man's ribs. The little goon doubled up with a wheezing gasp. Manning grabbed the lightweight hoodlum by the back of the neck and the seat of the pants to heave him into his fat partner.

The big guy unwittingly shoved his pal into a wall. Manning stepped forward and jabbed a left to Fatty's double chin. The thug's head bounced. Manning jabbed again and swung a right cross for the guy's jaw. The fat man surprised Manning and ducked. He charged low and slammed into Manning, his massive weight smashing the Canadian into the door. The heavyweight thug wrapped his arms around Manning's waist, pressurizing his ribs.

Continuing to squeeze, his opponent lifted him. The pain seemed to freeze Manning's lungs and cut off his breath. With a free arm, the Phoenix commando hammered a fist into the side of the other man's skull. Fatty grunted, but held on.

Manning raised both hands and clapped the open palms against the goon's ears. The fat man cried out. Manning gripped the man's ears with all eight fingers and slid his thumbs along the guy's cheeks. The thug moved his head back, afraid Manning would hook the thumbs into his eyes and gouge them from their sockets. The Canadian's thumbs found the guy's nose and shoved them into both nostrils. Manning pressed hard and dug his thumbs deeper. The goon's head moved back, eyes squeezed shut and teeth clenched in agony.

The fat man released Manning to attempt to yank the thumbs out of his nostrils. The Phoenix commando pulled them out first and slammed his forearms down on the other man's arms. He followed with a hell-of-the-palm stroke under his opponent's already aching nose. The guy's head recoiled, and blood seeped from his nostrils. Manning hit him with a left hook and spun the fat man around to receive a stunning blow from a ceramic lamp.

The skinny goon had grabbed the lamp from the bedside table, intending to use it on Manning, but smashed the improvised weapon down on the wrong man's skull. He was startled to realize he had clobbered his partner and watched the fat man collapse to the floor. Manning hooked a boot to the scrawny opponent's ribs and kicked him across the room. The guy hit a wall, bounced off and swung a wild kick for Manning's groin. The Canadian caught his opponent's foot and ankle in both hands. He twisted hard and shoved.

The man landed on the bed. The mattress slid off, and the thug landed on the floor. He tried to get up, but Manning kicked him in the ribs and slammed a hammer-first between his shoulder blades. The goon fell flat on his belly across the mattress. Manning planted a knee at the small of the guy's back and pinned him to the floor. Then he grabbed one arm and twisted it into a hammerlock. The Phoenix pro held the painful grip with one hand and seized his opponent's neck with the other. His fingers pinched off one carotid artery while the thumb pushed down on the other. The man struggled briefly, but the oxygen had been cut off from his brain and he soon passed out. Manning released the grip, not wishing to kill the guy or turn him into a brain-damaged vegetable.

The door burst open. Manning nearly launched himself at the figure in the doorway before he recognized Rafael Encizo. The Cuban had kicked the door open, Walther pistol in his fists. Encizo glanced about at the clutter in the room and the two unconscious figures.

"I thought I heard a ruckus in here," Encizo said as he raised his pistol to point at the ceiling. The P-88 does not have a safety catch, but there are built-in safety mechanisms in the trigger and firing pin design. He moved his finger from the trigger and slowly lowered the pistol. "Thought you might need some help."

"You might help me cuff these bastards," Manning replied.

The Cuban retrieved his briefcase from the hall. A curious hotel guest stuck his head out the door of his room, saw the gun in Encizo's hand and immediately disappeared back into his room. The Cuban commando opened the valise and removed two sets of plastic riot cuffs. He tossed one to Manning and headed for the fat guy to bind the man's wrists before he regained consciousness.

"If these two are with room service, I think you ought to complain to the management," Encizo remarked as he cuffed the obese thug.

"I found them searching the room," Manning explained. He cuffed the skinny goon and rose to his feet. "They both drew knives and came at me. Could be common thieves."

"Could be more than that," the Cuban said, studying a green and red snake tattoo on the fat man's forearm.

"I'm not sure, but I think this thing represents Damballah, the voodoo snake god. Might be an obeah symbol instead or something that doesn't have anything to do with either religion. Could just be a decoration and the guy likes snakes."

"They both likes snakes," Manning commented. He found a similar serpentine tattoo on the skinny guy's arm. "Seems a bit much for a coincidence, but I guess we shouldn't jump to any conclusions."

"We don't have to," the Cuban said with a sly smile. "Both of these guys are still alive. They can tell us what they were looking for."

There was a knock at the door, and it creaked open. Encizo had broken the frame when he kicked it in. Standing at the threshold, the desk clerk trembled slightly, fearful of what he might discover. The man was surprised to see Mr. Turner and another guest standing over a pair of characters who looked like riffraff of some sort. He glanced at the debris in the room, mouth open in astonishment.

"What on earth is going on here?" he asked. "A man with a gun was reported to be in this room."

"This is going to take some time to explain," Manning told him. "Don't worry. We're good guys, but now we'll have to tell you some things we had hoped to keep confidential."

"I don't know that I want to hear this," the desk clerk said nervously.

"I'm afraid you don't have any choice," Encizo informed him with an apologetic shrug.

8

Colonel Barama, Captain Takutu and George Sutcliffe were not pleased that the five mysterious commandos had summoned them to the Royal Inn. The Guyanese security and CIA had pulled a lot of strings and cut yards of red tape in order to set up airtight security for Phoenix Force and oblige them in just about every way possible. Now the hotshots with White House authority seemed willing to disregard all established procedures to arrange an emergency meeting at the hotel instead of at the safehouse.

They were surprised to find Gary Manning and Rafael Encizo seated in the lobby, waiting for them. No one else, except the desk clerk, was present. The restaurant was closed, and the hotel was very quiet at two o'clock in the morning. The Phoenix pair rose as Sutcliffe and the Guyanese officers entered the lobby.

"Colonel," Manning began, and turned to the desk clerk. "This is Mr. Acarai. He works here. We told him that we're in Guyana to investigate the massacre at the village for the United States government because Americans were involved in the incident."

"You told him *what*?" Sutcliffe demanded, stunned by the Canadian's announcement.

"We had to tell him in order to explain why we're authorized to carry firearms," Manning explained. "Mr.

Acarai was good enough to calm a hotel guest who noticed one of us with a pistol. Told him we're Interpol investigators. In return for this favor, I assured him a Guyanese military official of field-grade rank would confirm our claim."

"God Almighty, Turner," the CIA man groaned, and shook his head. "I can't believe you guys screwed up like this."

"Sorry," Manning said. "But it would have been a hassle if I let the two bastards I found in my room kill me. Somebody would have had to explain why I was murdered."

"Men in your room?" Barama asked with a frown. "What are you talking about?"

"I didn't call the police because they insisted this was a matter for national authorities," Acarai stated. "Is that correct, Colonel?"

"May I get an explanation first before I say anything one way or the other?" Barama said, an edge of frustration in his voice.

Manning and Encizo told them about the men Manning had found in his room. They were surprised, but unwilling to connect the incident with the mission. Barama suggested someone had sent the pair of goons to search Manning's room because they suspected he was more than a photojournalist.

"Where are these men now?" Captain Takutu asked.

"Upstairs with our other three partners," Encizo answered. "They're interrogating the scum. We should know whether they're common criminals or part of a conspiracy after the question-and-answer session is over."

"Captain," Barama began and turned to face Takutu. "I want you to talk to Mr. Acarai. Reassure him that security is necessary in this matter and that he has to keep this confidential. I'm going upstairs.''

"I can't believe you assholes pulled a stunt like this," Sutcliffe whispered to Encizo.

"Give your mouth a rest," the Cuban advised. "Let's just check on our partners' progress before anyone starts throwing accusations."

They mounted the stairs and headed for Calvin James's room. David McCarter, peering through the slightly open door into the hall, saw them approach and opened the door wide. He held an Uzi machine pistol and wore his Browning Hi-Power in shoulder leather.

"Aren't you overreacting?" Sutcliffe remarked, startled by the Briton's firepower.

"Not yet," McCarter assured him. "Keep it quiet, gents. The doctor's with his patients."

The two men were strapped to chairs inside the room. Katz sat at the foot of the bed, the steel hooks of his prosthesis laid across the open palm of his left hand. Moving from one captive to the other, Calvin James placed a stethoscope to each man's chest and consulted his wristwatch to time the subjects' heartbeats. He also checked the mercury sphygmomanometers attached to the prisoners' arms. James inspected the pressure cuff and bag of the blood pressure gear and watched the calibrated tubes of the gauges.

The fat man's head bowed forward on his chest, and the skinny fellow was sprawled back in his chair. Both men's eyes were closed, and they mumbled as if talking in their sleep. Katz and James asked the subjects questions in French. The captives replied with slurred words, their French laced with Creole expressions.

"What did you do to them?" Barama demanded, worried that he was witnessing some form of chemical torture.

"Keep it down," McCarter hissed. "They're being interrogated under the influence of truth serum. Scopolamine."

"Isn't that dangerous?" Sutcliffe asked. "I've heard about people dying from that drug."

"Mr. Brown knows what he's doing," Manning said, using James's pseudonym. "He's used scopolamine many times in the past and never lost a subject."

"If these men are just common burglars..." Barama began.

"Who just happen to be Ton Ton Macoute?" Katz stated as he rose from the bed and approached the colonel. "That's a bit much for a coincidence, wouldn't you say?"

"Ton Ton Macoute?" Sutcliffe's eyes widened. "You mean Duvalier's secret police in Haiti? I thought they were washed up when Baby Doc fled the country."

"The Ton Ton Macoute may not be an organized enforcement arm for any government," Katz replied. "But former members of Duvalier's storm troopers have found other ways to make a living with their skills for murder and brutality. We've seen ex-Ton Ton Macoute turn up in criminal syndicates and terrorist outfits. A lot of them fled Haiti after Duvalier left. Some even had enough sense to get out before the revolution in 1986."

"Those who stayed took the chance of being hunted down and killed by the people of Haiti," Encizo added. "I'm not going to shed any tears for any of those butchers. The Ton Ton Macoute more than deserves whatever they get."

"Don't you believe in arrest and trial?" Barama inquired.

"I believe in justice," the Cuban replied. "That doesn't always come from a courtroom."

James opened a leather packet and removed two syringes. He stuck one into a small vial and eased up the plunger to draw liquid into the syringe. The black commando gave the injection to one of the subjects and repeated the procedure for the other man.

"They'll sleep for about six hours and wake up with a royal headache," he announced. "No other ill effects, except I assume they'll find themselves in a jail cell when they come to."

"What did they tell you?" Barama asked.

"They said their boss is a former high-ranking Ton Ton Macoute team leader named Guillotin," James explained. "No shit. The guy really goes by that name. Since they left Haiti, Guillotin's gang of Ton Tons have been hiring out as mercenaries and assassins. Neither one of these bastards even knows how many people he's personally killed. I doubt either one of 'em can count past ten, but that's still a lot of innocent lives. Gives you some vague idea how many murders Guillotin's group could be responsible for."

"What were they doing in Turner's room?" Sutcliffe inquired.

"Guillotin ordered them to search Turner's room and Carver's, as well," James answered. "It seems whoever hired the Ton Tons was suspicious of them for some reason, but these two Haitian half-wits don't know why. Guillotin figured Turner and Carver might be cops or CIA. He just wanted the Mutt and Jeff of Ton Ton trash to look for evidence. He insisted they not carry guns because he wanted to discourage any confrontations."

"I'm sort of glad he did," Manning remarked.

"I bet those two aren't," Encizo commented, and tilted his head toward the captives. "What did they say about the massacre at the village?"

"That's the bad news," James said with a sigh. "These two turds don't know anything about it. They didn't even read anything in the newspapers concerning the incident. Of course, I figure they're functionally illiterate, anyway. They heard about it, but paid so little attention they didn't even know Senator Handel's kid was one of the people involved."

"How reliable is this truth serum?" Barama asked.

"Very reliable," James assured him. "The most reliable of any type of truth serum. It's almost impossible to resist the drug. Posthypnosis is probably the most effective method, and I'm trained in hypnotism. I can spot it when a subject goes into a hypnotic state. These suckers are telling the truth."

"Did they give any idea why Guillotin thought Carver and I might be police or CIA undercover agents?" Manning inquired. "This guy isn't suspicious of the rest of our group?"

"They didn't know why Guillotin was suspicious of you two, but apparently their boss didn't even know about the rest of us," James answered. "That's interesting, isn't it?"

"Very," Manning confirmed, glancing at McCarter, who nodded knowingly. "The only people Carver and I have met on our own since we arrived are Wilkens and his companions at the restaurant."

"What would a sugar plantation rancher have to gain from hiring the Ton Ton Macoute?" Barama wondered aloud.

"Beats me," James said. "Twiddle Dumb and Twiddle Dumber didn't mention Wilkens when we interrogated them."

"We might look into Mr. Wilkens's background, just in case," Katz suggested. "I also think you've waited long enough to tell the colonel the most important information we got from the prisoners."

"What's that?" Barama asked, his eyebrows raised.

"The Ton Ton Macoute have been involved in stirring up riots here in Guyana," James declared. "They've been attacking native Guyanese of East Indian descent. They vandalized mosques, Hindu shrines and Christian churches with predominantly Indian congregations. Just to make things more interesting, they also admitted there's a gang of Indian mercenaries—and I mean actually from India or maybe Nepal or Pakistan—who are carrying out identical types of assaults on black Guyanese communities and places of worship."

"These foreign toad scum are responsible for what's happened in my country in the last three days?" Barama demanded, his eyes suddenly bright with anger.

"That's how it looks," James confirmed. "It would explain all the racial violence and senseless attacks on churches, mosques and temples that erupted without any warning. It's been deliberate. These sons of bitches are purposely trying to get black and Indian Guyanese to turn against each other."

"Who would have anything to gain from this?" Sutcliffe asked. "It doesn't make sense."

"Perhaps we can squeeze more details from other members of this conspiracy," Katz suggested. "The prisoners told us that the Ton Ton Macoute and the In-

dian mercenaries have set up a base outside Georgetown. I think we should pay them a visit. Tonight.''

"It's already morning," McCarter commented.

"Before daybreak," Katz amended with a weary nod.

"Hold on," Sutcliffe began, hands raised to fend off
their arguments before they could even hear his state-
ment. "You guys are here on a mission concerning the
incident at the village and the murder of several American citizens, including the son of a U.S. senator. You are
not here to play Elliot Ness and the Untouchables,
charging around after every goddamn gangster in Guyana. This is not part of your mission."

"Isn't it a bit of a bloody coincidence all this shit hit
the figurative fan right after the village incident?"
McCarter inquired. "I don't know if these things are
connected, but I reckon we ought to find out."

"If there is a connection, we need to be on top of this
in order to investigate the scene and interrogate the enemy," Katz added. "Besides, we have to carry out the
raid as soon as possible because the Ton Ton Macoute
and their Indian counterparts will certainly assume these
two morons were caught trying to search the rooms of
Turner and Carver. That means they'll move to another
location as soon as they can."

"They probably wouldn't dream that anyone could get
information this quickly with truth serum," Barama remarked. "That should buy us enough time to put together at least a company of crack soldiers and police
officers for the raid."

"We don't know how far-reaching this conspiracy
might be," Manning warned. "The enemy could have
agents within the military and police. The best way to
maintain security is to handle this job ourselves."

"My God!" Sutcliffe exclaimed. "Are you guys nuts? You like taking on enormous odds? How many Haitian and Indian hoodlums are at this base?"

"We'll find out when we get there," Katz answered. "Let's go to the safehouse and get the rest of our gear."

9

Guyana is one of the largest producers of bauxite in the world. Bauxite is a soft mineral ore valuable for aluminum oxide, which is used in metal alloys. Aluminum, the most common metal on the earth's surface, is usually found in clay and granite compounds that are expensive and difficult to extract. Bauxite is found in pea-sized lumps, and the gibbsite and disaspore are easily refined for aluminum oxide.

The ravine south of Georgetown had been the site of a bauxite strip-mining operation. A set of iron tracks and a rusted old ore car were all that remained of the mining gear. The bauxite had been dug out from the hillsides years ago. The soil had suffered from the mining, and erosion had made the ravine worthless for farming. It had been long abandoned until the Ton Ton Macoute and the Nepalese mercenaries set up camp.

Phoenix Force observed the ravine from a forest of mora trees. Manning, peering through the Starlite night scope mounted to a Belgian-made FAL assault rifle, spotted two sentries, one posted on hilltops at each end of the quarry. The fiber optics of the Starlite magnified reflected light and created bizarre images in green and yellow, but Manning clearly saw both men were armed with rifles similar in design to his own FAL.

"Only two sentries posted above," he whispered to Katz and Colonel Barama. "I can't see into the ravine from this angle."

"No idea how many opponents are down there?" Barama whispered.

The Guyana Defense Forces had never been in actual combat with rival military forces. Except for the recent outbreak of riots, there had been no serious internal violence since the early 1960s. The British had sent troops to help restore order during the previous turmoil. Barama and his men had graduated from advanced combat and survival training, but they lacked experience. Barama, Captain Takutu and the five Guyanese paratroopers they had handpicked for the raid were battlefield virgins.

"How many opponents we have to deal with isn't as important as it would be under different circumstances," Katz replied. "If we can box them in the quarry, we'll have the advantage of the high ground. If they put up a fight, we can put them out of action by simply tossing tear gas and concussion grenades down on them. They'll have a difficult time trying to fire up at us from the bottom of the ravine."

"You make this sound easy," Takutu commented.

"It's never easy," Katz corrected, "and it's always dangerous. A raid like this can go wrong a hundred different ways. These things are unpredictable. Especially when we know relatively little about our enemies."

"We've gone after others knowing a lot less," David McCarter remarked as he peered through a Starlite scope mounted to a Barnett Commando crossbow.

"I don't recall any of those being a cakewalk, either," Calvin James muttered.

The Phoenix commandos had donned black night camouflage uniforms, paratrooper boots and matching headgear. The Guyanese troops were dressed in similar attire, but with the maroon berets or *pagris* of their paratrooper status. Only Barama and one of the enlisted men wore turbans instead of berets. Most of the men had smeared their faces and hands with burnt cork to blend better into the shadows. James and the black Guyanese did not need this additional camouflage.

They were all well armed. The Phoenix pros carried Uzi machine pistols. More compact than the famous submachine gun of the Israeli military, the Uzi's "little brother" was not as accurate and lacked the range of the larger weapon. But it was ideal for close-quarters combat that required rapid-fire destruction. The Phoenix Uzis fired semi-auto and 3-round bursts as well as full-auto. Manning and James were the best rifle marksmen of Phoenix Force. The Canadian favored the accuracy and knock-down power of the 7.62 mm FAL rifle. James carried an M-16, complete with foot-long silencer and Starlite scope.

McCarter's Barnett crossbow was a modern version of a centuries-old design. The skeletal metal stock and cocking lever made the Commando model more compact and faster to reload and fire bolts. His quiver included bolts with red or green feathered shafts. Red bolts contained lethal cyanide in the split fiberglass shaft near the steel tip. Green were nonpoisonous, used to wound instead of kill.

The Guyanese soldiers were armed with British L1A1 versions of the FAL assault rifle and Sterling Patchett submachine guns. Their side arms varied. Officers carried 9 mm NATO L9A1 Browning autoloaders and noncoms had Smith and Wesson .38 Special revolvers.

Phoenix Force and their South American allies also carried an assortment of grenades, knives, ammo pouches and protective gas masks in canvas cases.

Rafael Encizo climbed down from the branches of a mora tree and shinnied along the trunk to the ground. A pair of night-vision binoculars hung from the Cuban's neck. Katz handed Encizo an Uzi, and the Hispanic commando slipped the strap over his right shoulder.

"Did you see into the ravine from up there?" the Israeli inquired.

"After I climbed high enough," Encizo replied. "The branches seemed to get skinnier the higher I went. I began to wish I had a parachute. Anyway, I finally got a decent view of the enemy camp. There are four tents down there, each large enough to accommodate half a dozen men, maybe more."

"Let's assume the worst and figure there are about thirty of them," Katz stated.

"There are only a dozen of us," Barama reminded him.

"We can all count, Colonel," the Phoenix Force commander assured him. He turned back to Encizo. "Did you see anything else?"

"There are lights on inside one of the tents," Encizo answered. "Not everybody is asleep down there. A radio antenna is mounted outside that tent, so it's probable their communications center is located there. Could be the unit command post, as well. There are also two trucks in the ravine. Deuce and half, military rigs. I didn't see any guards posted below, but the two guys on the hills are an obvious problem. The forest extends beyond the quarry, so perhaps we can hit the enemy from both sides."

"All right," Katz said with a nod. "You, Carver and I and two of the Guyanese soldiers will move into position. Colonel Barama will stay on this side with the rest of his men. Your people will back up our team. If my people get in trouble, you can help them out of it. Agreed, Colonel?"

"You're in charge," Barama answered. His tone suggested he was more than willing to let Katz shoulder the responsibility.

"Give us ample time to get into position," Katz told the others. "We want to take out the sentries simultaneously and as quietly as possible, so as not to alert the enemy."

The assault force divided. Katz, Encizo, McCarter and two paratroopers headed through the forest to get into position at the opposite side of the quarry. Barama ordered his men to stay behind cover and wait. Manning aimed his FAL at a sentry. The cross hairs found the man's head, the center of the X marked the back of his skull.

"We have to wait," James whispered to the Canadian.

"I know," Manning said. "I just want to make sure I can take this guy out with one shot."

"I'm sure you can," James stated. "What worries me is the dude could fall off the hill and land in the camp below."

"There's a good chance that could happen," the Canadian admitted. "You want to do it the old-fashioned way?"

"Not really, but I don't see any other way," James said. He handed his M-16 to Barama. He couldn't hope to approach the sentry silently if he carried too much hardware.

James reached under his right armpit and drew the Blackmoor Dirk from its scabbard. Holding the Kraton rubber grip tightly, he glanced at the eight-inch, double-edged blade. Designed by Blackjack Knives, the dirk featured a top-notch stainless steel blade with a Rockwell hardness of fifty-eight degrees. He couldn't risk using a knife that might break if it hit a human rib or sternum.

"I'll cover you," Manning promised. "Be careful."

James nodded and slowly crept forward.

THE SECOND TEAM, led by Katz, made its way through the trees and into position at the opposite side of the quarry. They had also considered the problem of removing the sentry without having him fall into the ravine. Encizo, a veteran knife expert, grimly accepted his chore and approached the sentry, confident McCarter would have his crossbow ready if anything went wrong.

The Cuban made the most of available cover to conceal his approach. He crept cat-footed to a tree stump and crouched low. The sentry didn't seem to notice. He stared in another direction and kept his back to Encizo. The Cuban crept to a cluster of tall weeds and grass by a ledge. The ground was soft and shifted under his feet. The noise seemed very loud to Encizo, but he realized it was unlikely the guard would notice. He breathed slowly, silently through his open mouth. His heart raced.

Drawing closer, he clutched the pistol grip of the Uzi machine pistol. He did not intend to use the Uzi unless the sentry spotted him before he could get close enough to use the Cold Steel Tanto. The Cuban crept up the ridge and gradually peered around the corner. His opponent was still facing away from him. The sentry was short and stocky and appeared to be an East Indian or perhaps

Nepalese. An assault rifle was canted across the man's shoulder.

Encizo crept toward his target. His left hand moved to the knife sheath on his belt. The Velcro thumb strap was already open to avoid the telltale ripping sound. Encizo slid the Tanto from leather. The checkered neoprene grips of the handle were familiar in the Phoenix pro's hand. He had used the Cold Steel blade for several years. It had never failed him in combat.

The sentry moved his head. Encizo froze and pointed his Uzi at the man. The guard didn't look in his direction, but shuffled to a boulder and leaned against the rock, apparently fatigued or bored. Good, Encizo thought as he crept within ten yards of his target. The man would be less alert and easier to take out. He released the Uzi and swapped the Tanto to his right hand as he moved closer.

Suddenly the sentry swung around the boulder and laid the barrel of his assault rifle along the edge of the stone. The muzzle stared at Encizo. The son of a bitch had him cold. Encizo threw himself into the hillside and tried to flatten against it. He dropped the Tanto and grabbed the Uzi, aware his opponent could blast him before he could hope to use the machine pistol.

Something sizzled through the night air and landed with a solid thud. The sentry's head bobbed into view, a fiberglass shaft protruding from between the man's eyebrows. Red feathers bristled at the end of the crossbow bolt. McCarter's shot would have been fatal without the cyanide, but the poison dose to the brain ensured the man's death would be instantaneous. The sentry fell backward and slid down the hill, rifle still clenched in his lifeless fist.

"*¡Cristo!*" Encizo hissed under his breath as he watched the dead man plunge into the ravine.

The corpse hit the ground below. The impact jarred the dead man's rifle. A short burst of full-auto fire erupted from the quarry. Voices cried out in alarm in the enemy camp.

"*Merde alors!*"

The sentry on the far side of the quarry, a black Haitian armed with an FAL-style rifle, spotted Encizo and swung his weapon toward the Cuban. Another figure appeared behind the sentry. A tall, athletic black man pounced the Haitian. Calvin James grabbed the guard's throat with one hand and hammered the butt of his Blackmoor Dirk across the gunman's wrist to strike the rifle from his grasp. James pulled the guy back and drove the point of the dirk into the sentry's solar plexus, stabbing the sharp steel into the Haitian's heart.

As James pulled the slain sentry to a ridge, Encizo drew a concussion grenade from his web belt, pulled the pin and tossed it into the quarry. James also lobbed a grenade into the enemy stronghold. The other members of Phoenix Force and Colonel Barama's men charged from the forest.

The grenades exploded. The ground trembled as if gripped by a miniature earthquake. One of the tents collapsed, and enemy forces in the ravine scrambled. Several automatic weapons were fired at Encizo and James. Bullets raked the hills and splattered clumps of dirt on the two Phoenix commandos. Both retreated from the edge of the quarry and hurled more grenades at the enemy.

Explosions bellowed within the ravine. Another tent fell amidst cries of pain. The dirt walls of the quarry confined the force of the blasts. The Haitian and Ne-

palese mercenaries received a vicious hammering from
the grenades, but they were far from beaten.

Large projectiles, hurled from the quarry, sailed several hundred feet into the air. The Phoenix veterans recognized the threat and dove for cover. Some of the
Guyanese soldiers failed to realize the danger until the
projectiles fell to earth and exploded on impact. One
paratrooper was thrown two-dozen feet by a blast, his
clothes and flesh ravaged by shrapnel. Another explosion occurred directly in front of a soldier. His arms were
torn from their sockets, and his head popped off the stem
of his neck.

"They've got grenade launchers!" Manning shouted
for the benefit of the Guyanese. "Keep moving forward!
They won't fire the grenades too close to the rim of the
quarry, because they could bury themselves if the hills
crash down on them!"

"I sure as hell hope they realize that," McCarter
growled as he discarded his Barnett and grabbed his Uzi
with both hands.

They advanced on the ravine. An engine grumbled and
a truck rolled up the path of the quarry. Mercenaries ran
behind the truck for cover as they attempted to escape the
death trap in the quarry.

McCarter dashed to the road and cut off the truck. He
raised his Uzi and sprayed the windshield with 9 mm
slugs. Cracks appeared in the glass, as did several holes,
including three by the steering wheel. The driver slumped
behind the wheel. A merc in the passenger's seat pointed
a blue-black pistol out the window and fired at Mc-
Carter. The Briton dove to the ground as bullets slashed
through the air around him.

Gary Manning trained his FAL on the gunman in the
truck. Centering the cross hairs of the scope under the

mercenary's right shoulder blade, he squeezed the trigger. A 7.62 mm round punched into the man's back and drilled through his lung. The merc slid to the floor of the cab as the truck continued to roll forward.

Mercenaries at the rear of the rig swung their weapons at McCarter. A loud whistle startled the gunmen. They glanced toward the sound to see Katz's machine pistol pointed at them. The Israeli fired the Uzi and nailed the closest opponent in mid-chest with three 9 mm slugs. Dropping to one knee, Katz triggered a salvo as he slashed the Uzi in a diagonal motion. Three more mercs convulsed as bullets ripped into their abdomens.

Two of the gun-toting goons collapsed. Blood oozed from ruptured intestines and punctured stomachs. One man shrieked in a high-pitched wail. The third opponent, although doubled up from the bullet in the gut, still pointed his Beretta M-12 submachine gun at Katz. The Israeli triggered his Uzi again and blasted the merc's skull apart.

Another gunman poked a rifle around the edge of the truck and fired. Katz threw himself to the ground and rolled. A trio of tiny dirt geysers spat up from the ground less than a foot from where he had been.

The truck continued forward. The rifleman jogged alongside it to maintain his cover. More mercenaries were in the back of the rig. Two sliced portholes in the canvas tarp and thrust gun barrels through. Katz fired at the portholes and tore three bullet holes in the canvas. One gun barrel disappeared. The other tilted upward and released a short burst into the night sky.

"Watch yourself, mate!" McCarter shouted as he jogged forward and hurled a grenade in an underhand throw, a variation of a cricket pitch.

The grenade hit the ground and rolled under the truck just as he'd planned. The concussion blast lifted the rig. Tires left the ground, and the vehicle toppled over. The guy who was trying to use the truck for cover screamed as the big rig crashed down on him.

A Haitian gunman jumped from the rear of the truck and hit the ground in a desperate roll. Katz dashed forward to meet the merc before he could get to his feet. The Israeli booted a Beretta subgun from the Ton Ton Macoute thug's hand. In return the mercenary grabbed the Phoenix commander's ankle and twisted hard to try to throw Katz off balance. The Israeli slashed the Uzi across the man's skull. The Haitian released Katz's ankle and dropped to all fours, stunned.

"Behave yourself," Katz rasped, and kicked the guy behind the ear.

The Haitian fell unconscious at Katz's feet as a Nepalese mercenary emerged from the truck, pointing an FAL rifle at the Phoenix pro's back. Blood trickled into the killer's eyes from a scalp wound he had received when the truck spilled over. He blinked to clear his vision. Suddenly McCarter was beside him with an Uzi aimed at the Nepalese gunman's head.

"Drop it," the Briton snarled. "I won't tell you twice."

The mercenary let his rifle fall to the ground and began to raise his hands. Hoping McCarter was distracted, the thug whirled and grabbed for the handle of a *kukri* knife in a scabbard on his belt.

McCarter fired and blew the guy's head off.

RAFAEL ENCIZO HURLED an M-26 fragmentation grenade at a second truck as another group of mercenaries desperately tried to climb inside. Two Nepalese thugs dashed to the grenade in a frantic effort to scoop it up and hurl it out of the ravine. Others realized the folly of this action and ran from the vehicle. A Haitian had already climbed into the cab and started the engine. He wondered why the others seemed so panic-stricken. Voices shouted warnings in Nepali, Newari and Tamil, but not in a language the driver understood.

The grenade exploded as the two Nepalese hired guns tried to grab it. Both men were torn apart instantly. The blast's destruction swept over the truck. The deuce and a half erupted into a cluster of flying metal and wood debris. Gasoline ignited and set scraps of canvas ablaze. A flaming rag drifted through the air and landed on the head and shoulders of a fleeing mercenary. The man clawed at the burning fabric as his face and hair sizzled. His screams were stifled when he inhaled fire. He collapsed, more dead than alive, his throat scorched. Unconscious, the man suffocated on his own swollen and blistered tongue.

Phoenix Force and Barama's men lobbed tear gas grenades into the enemy camp, then donned protective masks. Exposed to the merciless fumes, half-blind, coughing and gagging, the remaining members of the mercenary forces were severely restricted in their ability to continue the battle.

Some were already unconscious from the concussion blasts. Others had suffered ruptured eardrums and sinuses. The few who had any strength left were unable to fight. A few charged from the mouth of the ravine and fired, although they could barely see their opponents.

Calvin James jogged to the ridge and jumped into the ravine behind two dazed mercenaries. He grabbed one by the back of the collar and jabbed him above a kidney with the stubby barrel of the Uzi. Then he slammed a knee into the man's tailbone and slapped the frame of his machine pistol across the guy's skull.

As the mercenary wilted senseless to the ground, his comrade turned to face James. The tough guy from Chicago unleashed a tae-kwon-do kick and booted the Beretta chopper from the merc's grasp. He followed the kick with a hard left hook to the jaw and stabbed his Uzi barrel into the man's belly. The mercenary doubled up with a groan, and James chopped his free hand across the side of the goon's neck. The man fell unconscious at the Phoenix warrior's feet.

Another pair of enemy troops, one Haitian and one Nepalese, headed toward the crippled truck beyond the ravine. Eyesight blurred by the gas, they triggered streams of full-auto fire at the vehicle. One of the Guyanese soldiers ran out of luck as three stray rounds split open his mask, punctured a lens to his headgear and blasted his skull apart.

Encizo fired at the pair. A trio of Uzi rounds tore between the shoulder blades of the Nepalese thug. His spine severed, the mercenary dropped his weapon and crumpled to the ground. The Haitian swung his weapon at the Cuban. Encizo dropped to a prone position along the ridge. His opponent's vision was too fuzzy to see the dark shape in the shadows. Encizo triggered his Uzi to pump three 9 mm slugs into the gunman's chest. The Haitian was knocked four feet by the impact. His body crash-landed in a lifeless heap.

McCarter charged forward toward a last opponent pinning his wrist and the rifle it carried to the ground with his boot. The Briton poked the muzzle of his Uzi against the man's skull. The mercenary released the rifle. Katz stepped forward and kicked the FAL away.

"You're the last, fella," McCarter told the man, his voice distorted by the rubber and plastic filters of his M-17 mask. "Alive or dead. It's up to you."

The man made no effort to resist as the Briton pulled his arms back and cuffed his wrists together at the small of his spine.

10

"Several Guyanese soldiers were killed in that little raid of yours," Sutcliffe declared as he paced the floor of the safehouse, gesturing wildly as if close to a nervous breakdown. "This had better be worth the loss of those lives or you five are going to find yourselves in deep shit. White House authority or not, you can't do this sort of crap and just walk away from it."

"Shut up, you pencil-pushing pain in the arse," McCarter snorted with disgust. "I'm tired of hearing it."

Katz leaned back in a folding chair and fixed a Camel cigarette between the hooks of his prosthesis. He reminded himself that Sutcliffe was, after all, unaccustomed to serious missions that involved genuine risk and dangers. The CIA case officer had attained his position at the American Embassy in Guyana because he was adept at keeping a low profile. Sutcliffe was a senior Company man, but the CIA obviously did not have a high opinion of him. That was why they had assigned him to a place where nothing was supposed to happen. Indeed, very little of international interest had occurred in Guyana since the Jonestown massacre. Until now.

"We found the source of the riots in Guyana," Katz reminded Sutcliffe. "That's important and will save innocent lives. It is sad that some of Barama's men were killed during the raid, but they were volunteers and they knew the risks involved. Every man in the military realizes he may have to put his life on the line in the service of his country."

"I'm concerned about an international incident!" Sutcliffe replied, his face beet red.

"Needn't worry about that," Katz assured him. "This is officially acknowledged as a raid by the Guyana Defense Forces. Only a handful of people will ever know we were involved. What's really important is a possible link between the village slaughter and the mercenary soldiers involved in the race riots."

"A link?" The CIA man frowned. "What sort of link?"

"For one thing, the mercenaries were armed with firearms designed and manufactured by Fabrica de Itajuba and Beretta, probably imported by Taurus," Gary Manning stated. "That means the guns came from Brazil. The ammo used was also IMBEL, the same as the cartridge we found at the village."

"That's no proof," Sutcliffe said, rolling his eyes with frustration. "You said before that the pistol used at the village to murder the Carlston girl was probably a German-made Luger or something."

"A Walther P-38," Manning corrected. His eyebrows knitted in concentration, turning over information in his mind. "A pistol made in Nazi Germany. German..."

"What is it, mate?" McCarter inquired. "You're thinking about something."

"German," The Canadian confirmed with a nod. "You remember those two muscle-bound guys at Wilkens's table? They claimed to be from the Netherlands Antilles. They didn't talk much, but I noticed something familiar about their accent. It didn't sound Dutch, and I think I know why. They spoke English with a German accent."

"Oh, hell," Sutcliffe rasped, and shook his head. "How can you tell? All those Teutonic languages sound alike."

"Really?" Katz, the master linguist, inquired. "You think English sounds like Norwegian?"

"What does English have to do with this?" the CIA man asked.

"English is the most widely spoken Teutonic language in the world," the Israeli explained. "German, Dutch and other Teutonic languages have distinctly different accents. Of course, these accents also vary from country to country and region to region, just as we find in English. The so-called High German accent spoken in Berlin is a different accent than Bavarian. Swiss German and the Alemannish dialect spoken in Liechtenstein are even more different."

"That's fascinating," Sutcliffe said without enthusiasm. "But it doesn't mean Turner is right about Wilkens's friends."

"I speak German fluently," Manning declared. "I spent some time in West Germany and participated in missions all over the country. I heard lots of different dialects and accents. Those two men with Wilkens spoke with a Bavarian accent."

"Maybe there are Dutch dialects that sound the same when a person speaks English," Sutcliffe suggested. "Or they may have learned English from someone with a Bavarian accent. I think you just don't like Wilkens and you're looking for a reason to go after the man. We've done a background check on him. Stanley Wilkens is a respected businessman and plantation owner. True, he might be a racist, but that doesn't make him a master criminal involved in some sort of secret plot to murder innocent people and stir up race riots. What's to be gained by that, anyway?''

"We may have come across something larger and more complicated than we expected when we arrived in Guyana," Katz began. "The mass murder at the village may be connected with the deliberate orchestration of the riots. We still don't know enough to have a definite motive for either incident, but there's only one reason anyone would be creating large-scale civil disturbances. That is for reasons of political power."

"Wilkens isn't a Communist or a Nazi or anything like that," the Company man said with exasperation. "He's a member of the People's National Congress, the major political party in Guyana. That's like saying he's a Democrat back in the U.S."

"Does he have any political aspirations?" McCarter asked.

"We didn't find any evidence of that," Sutcliffe replied. "Oh, he supports candidates and favors certain politicians. Henry Goddard seems to be his favorite. Wilkens pushed a lot of financial support behind Goddard and pulled some strings for the guy to get his seat in the Guyanese National Assembly."

"You say he 'pulled strings,'" Manning noticed. "What does that mean?"

"Well, the National Assembly consists of fifty-three elected representatives and twelve appointed officials," Sutcliffe explained. "Goddard was appointed after Wilkens rallied support for him among other large landowners and trade exporters. This isn't really unusual in politics, especially in South America. Goddard is sort of an unusual candidate for the National Assembly in Guyana because he's white. Another successful native of

European descent. I suppose Wilkens's support had a lot to do with Goddard's appointment. He figured the guy would be more sympathetic toward fellow Caucasians. You want to call that racist, that's fine. Of course, you could say the same about blacks who supported Jesse Jackson when he ran for President.''

"Could be more behind it than just favoring his own race," Katz remarked as he fired up his cigarette and took a deep puff. "What's the public think of Goddard?"

"No major complaints that I know of," Sutcliffe said. "Hell, I didn't check *his* background. As far as I can tell, both black and Indian Guyanese seem to like him because he doesn't favor either group and hasn't done any special favors for whites. If Wilkens is getting any benefits from his association with Goddard, it's a well-kept secret."

"Nobody helps another person get into a high political office without wanting something in return," Manning commented.

"So, we all vote for candidates who express views we agree with," the CIA man said with a sigh.

"And hope they won't turn out to be lying about their position on those subjects," McCarter added with a disgusted snort. "Bloody politicians are always professional liars. Never know what the bastards will do after they get in office."

Rafael Encizo entered the bay area from a side door. The Cuban had caught only the end of McCarter's comment and figured the Briton was complaining about what crooks politicians are. Encizo shared that view but didn't feel like getting into a debate. The Cuban headed for the coffee maker and helped himself to a cup.

"Barama and his men have locked up the surviving members of the mercenary crew," Encizo announced.

"Mr. Brown is going to interrogate some of them with scopolamine after Barama can find some translators to communicate with these scum."

"Translators?" Sutcliffe asked with surprise. "I know the Haitians speak Creole French, but aren't the others East Indians? Don't they speak Hindi, or Urdu or some other language that's fairly common here?"

"They're not Indians," Encizo stated. "Most of them are Nepalese, and a few are from Sri Lanka."

"Sri Lanka?" The CIA man was astonished by this claim.

"Yeah," Encizo replied. "That's a fairly small country off the tip of India. Used to be called Ceylon."

"I have a vague idea where it is," Sutcliffe said dryly. "How did mercenaries from Sri Lanka and Nepal wind up in Guyana?"

"Their leader brought them here," Encizo explained. "They call him Captain Ajmer. He's supposed to be from a long line of Gurkha warriors. A family tradition. Sort of a Nepalese samurai."

"I'm getting really tired of the way you guys answer questions," Sutcliffe said, clearly frustrated. "Why did they do this?"

"Maybe they'll reveal more details when they're questioned with the truth serum," Encizo answered. "A few of them seemed willing to talk, but most clammed up. I wouldn't get my hopes up that these fellas will have much information. They're basically grunts. They follow orders, collect their pay and keep their mouths shut."

"I don't suppose we were lucky enough to nail either Ajmer or the Haitian leader, Guillotin," Manning remarked. He wasn't asking a question—the answer seemed obvious.

"Neither man was at the camp when we hit it," Encizo confirmed. "Maybe the camp commanders could have told us something. They ranked higher and probably knew more details about their mission in Guyana. Unfortunately none of them survived."

"This job is never easy," Manning commented. "Their weapons came from Brazil, no doubt through black market sources. Maybe the same used by the people who murdered the people at the village. Now, we know from personal experience there is a certain degree of truth to the stories of secret Nazi strongholds in South America. Especially in the Amazon jungle."

"I've heard stories for years that Martin Bormann is supposed to be hiding out somewhere in the Matto Grosso," Sutcliffe stated. "Now, you're not telling me Hitler's aide is still alive down there? The son of a bitch would have to be about ninety years old."

"It's unlikely Bormann is still alive," Katz said. "In the early 1970s a skull found in West Germany was officially recognized as that of Martin Bormann. There's always a chance the dental records are forged. However, whether Bormann escaped to South America is beside the point. A number of other Nazis did flee here after the war. Eichmann, Barbie, Mengele and others were found in this part of the world. On a previous mission, we encountered a Nazi stronghold run by Kurt Mohn, the son of a major in the SS. They were involved in cocaine smuggling and a scheme to use biochemical weapons. We can't give you many more details about Mohn's operation, but believe me, the Third Reich isn't as dead and buried as most people think."

"Next you'll tell me Hitler's not really dead," Sutcliffe muttered.

"They never found his body," McCarter remarked with eyebrows raised. "Did they?"

"Okay, Sutcliffe," Manning began. "I'll grant you this theory seems far-fetched and we don't have enough facts to back it up, but let's just say for a moment that Nazis in Brazil are involved in a gun-smuggling racket. Wilkens is a Nazi sympathizer or maybe even a Nazi himself."

"He's not German!" Sutcliffe insisted. "His father came to Guyana from England during World War II."

"Maybe his old man was actually a double agent for Abwehr Intelligence or Wilkens became a Nazi when he got involved with them as a youth," Manning continued. "Just let me finish. The Nazis got the weapons to Wilkens, and he hired these mercenaries from Haiti and Nepal to stir up racial tensions in Guyana. There were riots in 1962 and '63. Wilkens was here then. He was a kid at the time, but he certainly remembered. He knows he can start this sort of violence again, and people will think it's just the blacks and Indians fighting each other over racial differences and religion."

"But what does Wilkens get out of this?" Sutcliffe asked.

"Well, if the blacks and Indians learn to hate and distrust each other badly enough," McCarter mused, "a leader who doesn't represent either ethnic group might be regarded as the best choice for all involved. Especially a bloke who is fairly well liked by both sides of the conflict. Somebody like Wilkens's crony in the National Assembly."

"That's insane," the CIA man groaned. "The president and prime minister of Guyana aren't going to just resign from office and let Goddard take over."

"What if they're both dead?" Encizo inquired. "If Wilkens is ruthless enough to do all the rest, he won't draw the line at political assassination. Think of it. If they're both killed and all the evidence suggests it was done by black or Indian extremists, that would be even more motivation for Goddard to take control of the country. Wilkens calls off the mercenaries, and the riots stop after a while. That would sure make Goddard look good. Wouldn't it?"

"You guys ought to be making brooms for a living because you're so good at grasping for straws," Sutcliffe remarked. "Before we advise the heads of state in Guyana that their lives are in jeopardy, maybe you can explain one little item."

"How the mass murder at the village fits the rest of this theory?" Katz guessed what the Company man was going to say.

"You got an answer to that one?" Sutcliffe asked.

"Maybe it was done to try to sever relations with the United States in order to create economic troubles in Guyana," McCarter suggested. "Another miracle for Goddard to perform when he takes office."

"I don't think so," Katz replied. "Guyana doesn't do that much trade with the United States. Trying to hurt relations with Venezuela or Great Britain would probably work better, if that was the goal. Why pick a target that would insure the CIA and the NSA would be called in to investigate? There has to be another reason."

"Be sure to tell the rest of us if you figure it out," Sutcliffe said sarcastically.

OTTO WEISSFLOG ALSO HELD an emergency meeting in his den at the plantation. His son, Gerhart, Werner and Reinhard joined Weissflog to meet Captain Ajmer and

Guillotin. The stocky Gurkha and the big Haitian were angry and clearly upset with their employer.

"They attacked our base near Georgetown," Ajmer stated. "Thirty-two of our people were either killed or captured."

"And we know how the other side found out," Guillotin added grimly. "They learned the location from the two men I sent to investigate Turner and Carver at the Royal Inn. That's the only way they could have found out about our camp."

"Too bad your men are so incompetent," Gerhart remarked.

"My Ton Ton Macoute have considerably more experience in these matters than you, young man," Guillotin hissed, furious that someone so young dared to criticize him or his Haitian followers.

"They have experience in killing unarmed peasants," Gerhart scoffed. "They obviously couldn't handle opponents who can shoot back. They were also too stupid simply to search the hotel rooms of the two men my father suspected might be CIA agents."

"Your son could use some lessons in manners," the Haitian told Otto Weissflog, his eyes burning with anger.

"Don't insult our guests," Weissflog told Gerhart. "I taught you to have respect for your elders."

"Even when they're not my equals?" Gerhart muttered.

"Wait outside, Gerhart," his father said in a hard voice. "I see you're not mature enough to handle this sort of meeting."

"But, Father..." Gerhart began. Realizing his protests would not help, he turned on his heel and marched from the den.

Weissflog heard the door slam. Werner and Reinhard frowned. They didn't approve of reprimanding the lad for talking back to a black man. Weissflog wasn't concerned with their opinion. This was not a good time to increase the antagonism felt by the mercenaries toward their Nazi employers.

"Children can often be a problem," Captain Ajmer commented. "My son is quite an embarrassment to me. He became a Buddhist and entered a monastery near Katmandu. I blame it on his mother. She was a bad influence."

"How sad," Werner whispered sarcastically.

"What's done is done, and we'll have to continue this operation, accepting the reality of what has happened," Weissflog stated. "One thing we have learned is that my suspicions about Turner and Carver are correct. They must be CIA. Unfortunately they caught your men in the rooms."

"I don't know how they got my men to talk so quickly," Guillotin admitted. "I wouldn't have thought they would break so fast."

"Maybe they used drugs," Weissflog said with a shrug. "What's important is whether or not this raid means the rest of us are in jeopardy."

"We've already moved our other camp," Ajmer related. "A precaution in case the enemy forces captives to tell details about us. You're still safe, Mr. Wilkens. No one at the base knew anything about you. Guillotin and I will have to maintain a very low profile because they'll certainly find out about us if they're using some sort of truth serum."

"I wouldn't say any of us are truly safe at this point," Weissflog cautioned. He leaned back in his chair and glanced down at the ink blotter on his desk as if searching for information written there. "I have contacts in the police department and the military, as well as the National Assembly. None of them know anything about the raid. That means whoever did this was able to take action very quickly and maintain tight security on the raid. The only way that could be done is by using a minimum number of people for the mission. Twenty men, perhaps. They may have used even fewer for the job."

"Gut Gott!" Reinhard exclaimed. "They must be very brave to take on a base against superior odds. Perhaps they did not suspect how many opponents they would have to face."

"They probably knew they'd be outnumbered, but they accepted the risk," Weissflog stated. "These people have more than courage. They must also be very skilled. Very dangerous."

"They had the advantage of surprise," Ajmer remarked. "That can make a great difference. The ravine was not the best site to defend. I had doubts about that choice from the beginning."

"Too bad you kept that opinion to yourself," Guillotin remarked dryly. "If our problem consists of a small number of people, the solution seems obvious. We kill them."

"That might have worked for your Ton Ton Macoute when you were above the law in Haiti," Werner said with disgust. "But this is Guyana, and Baby Doc isn't in charge here."

"Do you have a better suggestion?" Guillotin demanded. "These foreigners you suspect are CIA must be some sort of special strike team. Something like Delta Force, the antiterrorist unit. The American government won't admit they even have a team like that, much less that they sent it to Guyana. They worry about their public image too much. If we kill them, Washington won't even whisper a complaint.''

"Perhaps," Weissflog said thoughtfully. "One thing my sources with the police in Georgetown did learn is the bodies of that senator's son and his girlfriend were discovered.''

"The youths the newspapers claim had been kidnapped?" Ajmer asked with surprise. "I thought you said they were dead and buried.''

"We had to bury them because they wouldn't pass as poison victims of mass suicide," Weissflog explained. "They tried to run. I had to chase them down on horseback to catch them. Killed the boy with my saber, but the girl made it to the jungle and I couldn't follow her on the horse. I had to shoot the little bitch.''

"They probably would have found the bodies eventually," Ajmer said. "No one has told the press about this?''

"Apparently not," Weissflog confirmed. "But the most interesting item is that a black American participated in the autopsies. Another man helped with ballistics. He was described as a white man from Canada or the United States. Sounds like our friend Mr. Turner. I'd say these two and our British friend, Mr. Carver, are all members of the same team. No doubt there are others, but this gives us a place to start.''

"Start what?" the Haitian asked, palms outstretched in an exaggerated gesture of helplessness.

"To start killing them of course," the Nazi leader replied, as if the answer was obvious. "I'll alert my informants to keep their eyes open for any of these bastards. If they give us the opportunity, we'll kill them all.''

"Our people can't mingle with Guyanese without drawing suspicion," Ajmer reminded Weissflog. "They may look like Indians, but most of them don't speak Hindi or other dialects from India. Their accent will expose them as Nepalese or Tamils from Ceylon."

"Don't worry," Weissflog assured him. "I'll take care of this. This mission has gone too far to stop now. I'm not going to allow anyone to get in my way. Those men are as good as dead."

11

A giant anteater stood at the edge of the dirt road. Nearly four feet long from the tip of its long slender snout to the end of its shaggy tail, the anteater was an odd-looking beast. A long sticky tongue slithered from its tiny mouth and licked up dozens of black ants. The insects rushed from the opening of their mound to defend it from the invader. This played directly into the primitive strategy of the anteater.

The tongue burrowed into the mound and drew out dozens more insects. The anteater devoured them in a mechanical, instinctive manner. A primitive but highly specialized mammal, it had been designed by nature to do little more than what its name implied. However, its food supply was always plentiful in Guyana. Relatively few animals fed on ants, so the mammal had little competition. It used its powerful front claws to tear apart the mound and gobble up more insects.

The anteater was so busy feeding it paid no attention to the slight tremor as two Land Rovers rolled across the road. The anteater raised its long sleek head. The animal's eyesight was poor, but it heard the approaching vehicles and lumbered into the tall grass.

"Now, that is one weird-looking critter," Calvin James remarked when he glimpsed the shaggy beast.

"We seldom see the giant anteater away from the heart of the rain forest," Siam Doraku stated. "It is an unusual animal."

"Nobody can argue with that," the American agreed. He glanced back at the second Land Rover and saw Captain Takutu behind the wheel, with Gary Manning seated beside him.

Doraku drove the lead Land Rover. He was a slender Indian youth, barely twenty-one years old, and apt to ramble during a conversation. Doraku had been born and raised in a village in the area of the mass murders that had led to Phoenix Force's mission in Guyana. The youth had moved to the small city of Tumatumari where he worked as a truck driver.

Colonel Barama and his investigators had learned about Doraku when they checked possible leads from villagers and former villagers familiar with the region. Most were reluctant to talk to outsiders, but Doraku had been eager to cooperate. When asked if he knew of any unusual incident that might shed light on the mystery of the Jonestown-style deaths, Doraku had an intriguing story to tell.

One year earlier, Doraku had ventured several miles from his village to meditate alone and decide whether he ought to leave the little farming community or live out his life in the village as most of the children born there had done. Doraku yearned to see more of the world, but he was reluctant to betray the people of his village by leaving.

The youth's meditation was disturbed by a sudden eruption of gunshots. Frightened, he hid in the jungle behind some large ferns as the shooting drew closer. Several uniformed men appeared, carrying "military guns"; Doraku did not think they were Guyanese soldiers, because they were white. Two figures on horse-back also appeared. Doraku clearly recalled a man on a black horse. He was tall and fierce, clearly in command as he snapped orders to the others in a strange language. He thought it was a European tongue, as some words were similar to English.

Doraku had remained hidden until the men with the guns departed. He told his father about the incident. The old man advised him not to speak of it. It is wise to avoid men in uniforms, his father warned. The governments and militaries were not regarded as the friends of small villages in the rain forest. It could even be dangerous to speak of such things. Doraku followed his father's advice. Although he left the community two months later, he had not told anyone else what he saw in the jungle until Barama's people contacted him in Tumatumari.

"WE'RE NEARLY THERE," Doraku announced as he brought the Land Rover to a halt. "We can't take this car the rest of the way. Have to go on foot, Mr. Brown."

"Okay," James agreed, and leaned over his seat to gather up his field jacket and Uzi machine pistol.

Doraku was nervous about the guns. James, who also carried a Walther P-88 pistol in shoulder leather under his left arm and a Blackmoor Dirk in a sheath under the right, climbed from the Land Rover and adjusted his sunglasses. The morning heat was already uncomfortable and threatened to worsen.

"You really don't need that jacket," Doraku told him.

"I need the pockets," James replied as he reluctantly slipped into the field jacket. He slid the strap of the Uzi over his right shoulder.

Doraku frowned. "You don't need those guns, either."

"I hope you're right about that," the Phoenix warrior replied. "But there's a saying about guns. It's better to have one and not need it than to need one and not have it. Just think of 'em as insurance, in case those dudes you saw last year show up again."

The other Land Rover halted, and Manning and Takutu emerged and approached James and Doraku. The Canadian wore khakis, paratrooper boots and a field jacket identical to James's. Manning carried an Uzi machine pistol and a "butt pack" at the small of his back. Takutu was armed with a Patchett submachine gun, with a 34-round box magazine inserted in a mag well located in front of the trigger guard.

"We have about five kilometers to walk into the jungle," Doraku explained as he pointed into the rain forest. "Then I can show you where I saw the soldiers...or whatever they were."

"Okay," Manning said, shrugging. "Let's do it."

They marched into the jungle. Monkeys chattered from the branches of greenheart trees. The small primates leaped from limb to limb and climbed higher to watch the men from a safer perch. Manakins and sugarbirds shrieked as the four intruders ventured into the rain forest. The canopy of leaves provided welcome shade as the men trekked through the foliage.

Gary Manning enjoyed the trip. Many people think of a jungle or tropical rain forest as a green hell. Manning had never found any jungle to be hellish. This view was not shared by some of his fellow Phoenix Force commandos, but Manning regarded the rain forests as a variation of the woodland areas he recalled fondly from his childhood.

Nature, alive and green and abundant with animals, never seemed like a hell to the Canadian. The insects were often a concern, and the heat and humidity might be sweltering, but Manning could accept those hardships. The simple beauty and drama of nature without human technology intruding always pleased Manning.

"Man, this is another damn hellhole," James muttered as he crushed a mosquito on his neck. The crimson smear on his palm revealed the insect had already drawn blood. "Like freakin' Vietnam again."

Manning kept his opinion to himself.

They continued to trudge through the rain forest. Ironically Takutu seemed the most awkward in the jungle environment. Although a native Guyanese, he was the product of a city and unaccustomed to the rain forests of his own country. The two Phoenix veterans had spent many hours in other jungles throughout the world. Previous missions had taken them to India, Mexico, Brazil, Colombia, the Philippines and three African countries, which all required some time in rain forests. Doraku, of course, had spent most of his life in the Guyanese jungles and found the setting perfectly normal.

Doraku stepped around a fallen, rotted log. Manning and James followed. Takutu began to step over the log, but James warned him that snakes, scorpions and other creatures sometimes make a home in such old logs. Takutu immediately backed away from the log and shuffled around it.

More than an hour later, they reached the area in which Doraku claimed he had seen the mysterious gunmen a year earlier. The Phoenix pair walked into the clearing and began searching through the tall grass. Takutu asked what they were looking for.

"Anything that might help us identify those men," Manning answered. "I know there may not be much left after a year. We're not going to find any footprints or hoofprints clear enough to match any of those left at the site of the mass murders. Too much time has passed, and the way plant life grows in this climate, it'll be hard to find any trace of anyone who was here a year ago.''

"We'll be lucky if we can find anything," James said in a resigned tone. "Maybe we'll have better luck if we try the spot where the guys were firing their weapons. Perhaps they didn't pick up all the brass or left some C-ration cans behind or something like that. We really won't know until we look."

"I'm beginning to think this isn't such a good idea," Captain Takutu remarked.

"Well, we interrogated those Haitian and Nepalese prisoners last night and didn't learn much more about them than we knew before the raid," James reminded him. "We've got a couple other leads to check on after this. Maybe this will pan out and maybe it won't. If it doesn't, we'll move on to the next. But let's not write this off until we give it a try."

"Most of the shooting seemed to come from the east," Doraku declared. "That way. Toward the river."

They had no success searching the clearing, so they moved in the direction Doraku suggested. The terrain was densely covered by greenheart trees, hanging vines, giant ferns and other plant life. Another hour passed, and the effort seemed hopeless until James discovered some rusted brass casings under a cluster of weeds.

"Jackpot!" he announced as he picked up three old cartridge casings. "Got about a dozen of these suckers here."

Manning joined him and gathered up more spent brass. He scraped rust from the rim and primer. IMBEL was stamped on the ammo shell housing.

"More Brazilian cartridges," the Canadian confirmed. "These are 7.62 caliber. Probably fired from FAL rifles produced by the Fabrica de Itajuba factories in Brazil."

"Assault rifles," Takutu said grimly. "You think there might be bodies buried here somewhere?"

"Maybe," James replied. "The problem is there are so many animals and insects in this rain forest there may not be anything left. Scavengers probably got it by now. Maybe we can find some bones, but trying to figure out where to start digging is gonna be just short of impossible."

"And probably unnecessary," Manning added as he found some more brass, including an unfired cartridge. "There's a live round here. Probably jammed in the rifle, and the guy jacked it out of the breech to clear his weapon and forgot to retrieve it."

James examined the shell. The tip was crimped and abbreviated. The American frowned for a moment, but his eyes soon widened as he realized the importance of the discovery.

"I'll be a son of misbegotten junkyard dog," he muttered. "This is a goddamn blank."

"Blank ammunition?" Takutu asked, puzzled by the find. "Why would they be shooting blank ammo?"

"They weren't shooting a movie here," Manning stated. "So there's only one other explanation. The men Siam saw in the jungle last year were conducting a training exercise."

"War games in preparation for genuine battle," James added. "Now we know why all those people were killed at the village and the other incidents were supposed to look like crazies left over from Jonestown."

"We do?" Takutu did not grasp this discovery.

"The men who conducted the war games wanted their training to remain secret," Manning explained. "Occasionally they got too close to individuals or villages not on the maps. They didn't want witnesses, so they killed them and made it look like deranged followers of the People's Temple had done it. Guyana doesn't want Jonestown dragged up again. The incident made your country famous, but it was hardly the kind of attention any nation would appreciate."

"It certainly wasn't," Takutu admitted. "So, all those people were killed to cover up training exercises? Even the U.S. senator's son?"

"Bob Handel and his group were just in the wrong place at the wrong time," James affirmed. "He wasn't killed for political reasons—not concerning the United States, anyway."

"But who were these men?" Doraku inquired. "Why were they carrying out these training exercises?"

"They're a paramilitary outfit," Manning answered. "They're preparing for combat because they want to be ready to fight anyone who objects to their planned takeover in the future."

"You still believe in that Nazi theory?" Takutu asked.

"Siam said they were white men who spoke an unfamiliar European language," Manning insisted. He turned to the youth and said, *"Sprechen sie Deutsch? Was bedeutet das?"*

"Yes," Doraku said with a nod. "That sounds like the language they spoke. What is it?"

"German," Manning declared. "I think we know who we're after now. It's just a matter of proving it."

"I don't understand," Doraku admitted.

"Unfortunately we can't tell you any more than we already have," James said. "A lot of this stuff has to stay confidential, and we may never be able to tell you all the details. Still, you'll know how things turn out—more or less.''

"And you will be rewarded for your assistance," Takutu assured him. "We'll see to that."

Manning heard leaves rustle to the west. He glanced over his shoulder and saw a figure dressed in a tan uniform duck behind the trunk of a large greenheart. The Canadian only glimpsed the man, but he was sure he had a gun. Manning immediately pushed Doraku off balance. The youth yelped with surprise as he hit the ground.

"Ambush!" the Canadian warrior shouted as he jumped behind the closest tree for cover.

James dove to the ground and shoulder-rolled to another tree trunk. Captain Takutu grabbed his Patchett chopper and glanced about for the threat that had spurred the Phoenix pair into action. Too late, he realized he needed to get to cover. Two submachine guns snarled from the bushes. Takutu's body twisted in a wild spasm as bullets crashed into flesh. His arms flew apart, his back arched and blood streamed from his torso and back.

The captain bellowed, then stumbled backward. Blood spurted from his punctured heart and splashed his shirt-front. More enemy rounds smashed into Takutu and drove him back into the tree Manning used for cover. The Canadian heard Takutu moan and the liquid gurgle as blood bubbled up from his throat and filled his mouth. Manning heard the scraping sound as the Guyanese officer slid down the trunk to the base of the tree.

Calvin James thrust his Uzi around the mora tree he had hastily selected for cover. The American pointed the machine pistol at the muzzle-flash of the killers' subguns.

He fired the Uzi one-handed, spraying the bushes to compensate for being unable to take better aim with two hands.

Parabellum slugs raked the bushes. One gunman screamed and fell forward, clasping his bullet-wrecked face and forehead. The uniformed figure collapsed lifeless, blood spilling between the fingers still held across his butchered features. Yet there was no doubt the gunman had been a white man, about twenty-five years old.

Bullets chipped bark from the mora tree near James's head. The black hardass from Chicago drew back behind the trunk. The shots came from a different direction than the bushes where the first two opponents had opened fire on Takutu. James scanned the surrounding area, aware any sensible opponent would try to hit them from multiple directions.

Siam Doraku rose and bolted to another tree. The enemy fired at the youth, but his unexpected run caught them off guard. Doraku was incredibly lucky. Bullets tore up dirt by his rushing feet and sliced air near his limbs and head, yet not one struck him.

Doraku's panicked run for cover effectively drew enemy fire and diverted attention from the Phoenix Force commandos. Manning took advantage of the distraction to open his butt pack and remove a couple of ounces of C-4 plastic explosives. The demolitions pro jammed the C-4 into the base of the greenheart. He took a pencil detonator from his jacket pocket. A special blasting cap and a timer dial were built into the device. Manning set the timer to ten seconds, inserted the detonator in the explosive and bolted from cover.

He ran with his back low and knees bent. The Canadian fired his Uzi at the bushes where he knew one enemy gunman was concealed. The opponent suddenly stood up behind the bushes, a Beretta M-12 subgun in one fist. His other hand clutched two bleeding holes in his chest. The guy's Nordic blue eyes expanded in amazement as he realized he had been shot through the heart. Aware he was dying, the man was too stunned to return fire and simply toppled to the ground.

The Canadian reached the cover of another tree as a volley of automatic fire erupted from a cluster of giant ferns. Bullets passed near the back of his neck, and one actually clipped his jacket collar. The commando's stomach was knotted by fear as he ducked beside the tree trunk. Two more slugs blasted holes in the wood above his bowed head.

James aimed his Uzi at the ferns and triggered a burst of 9 mm lethal messengers. Chunks of plant hopped from the stalks, severed by bullets. A scream announced that human flesh had also been hit. The wounded gunman staggered away from the ferns, an FAL rifle in one fist. James nailed him with three more Uzi rounds and the bastard went down for keeps.

Sparks snapped along the frame of James's Uzi. The force of the high-velocity slugs ripped the machine pistol out of his hands and sent it hurtling. The commando gasped and pulled back. His fingers trembled and ached from having the weapon abruptly wrenched from his grasp. It had also scared the hell out of him, and he was relieved to find he still had all ten fingers. James's little finger of his left hand was abbreviated at the tip, a memento of a nightmare session in a torture chamber during a previous mission. He did not want any more digits shortened.

"This is gettin' pretty hairy, man!" James exclaimed as he reached inside his jacket and drew the Walther pistol from shoulder leather.

"I left a surprise!" Manning shouted. "Be ready for it..."

The C-4 charge exploded. The blast uprooted the tree and sent it tumbling down. It crash-landed into the foliage, its branches slamming into another tree. Two enemy gunmen opened fire, irrationally shooting the tree as if it were human. They had reacted to the sudden movement and responded as though it was an attack.

Manning had hoped for this response, gambling that the enemy was relatively inexperienced in actual combat. The frenzied pace and general confusion on the battlefield are seldom conveyed in training exercises, which are carefully orchestrated and controlled to avoid injury.

He fired. One gunman went down with a trio of bullets in his chest. Another returned fire with a Beretta chopper. Kneeling, Manning used the tree for a post rest and fired the last rounds from his Uzi. Bullets slashed foliage near the enemy triggerman and drove the guy from the bush.

"Hey, butthead!" James called out as he trained the sights of his P-88 on the man's chest.

The gunman spat out an angry curse in curt German and raised his M-12. James's Walther pistol punched two 9 mm slugs into the bastard's chest. The goon fell backward, his Beretta subgun blasting branches and leaves overhead. He landed against a tree trunk and slid face-first to the ground.

A grenade sailed from a batch of large ferns and landed less than a yard from Calvin James. The black warrior immediately kicked it back in the direction from which it had come. He threw himself to the ground and hugged the base of the mora for as much shelter as possible. Two rifle rounds plowed into the ground near his legs and splattered dirt across James's prone form.

The grenade exploded. A loud groan ensued as a bloodied figure tumbled from the cover of the ferns. An FAL assault rifle clattered to the ground beside the battered form. James glanced about for signs of other opponents. Doraku stepped from cover, but Manning shouted to the youth to get his ass back to the tree and stay down.

"Keep an eye peeled!" James called out as he slowly approached the wounded figure who had been ravaged by the grenade blast.

James pointed his Walther at the man and carefully stepped closer. The enemy had been badly injured by shrapnel. One leg had been torn off at the knee, and blood flowed from wounds in his torso and chest. The American knelt by the man and pointed the P-88 at the guy's skull while he used two fingers of his free hand to check for a pulse at the carotid artery. He found none.

"Hell," James muttered. "I wanted to take one of these suckers alive."

"Better than them taking us dead," Manning remarked as he walked to the bullet-butchered corpse of Captain Takutu. "Not that all of us survived. Siam?"

"I am all right," the youth replied, and staggered forward on trembling legs. "I think these may have been some of the men I saw here last year."

"No kiddin'?" James replied sarcastically. The commando searched the pockets of the man killed by the grenade. "No dogtags, wallet, no ID of any kind. Nothing to suggest who these slime-buckets were working for."

"We must be getting closer to finding out, or these cretins wouldn't have attacked us," Manning declared.

"Let's get back to the road. We can use a radio in one of the Land Rovers to contact Barama. He ought to know what's happened."

"Yeah," James agreed. "Bad news can't wait."

12

Colonel Barama frowned as Calvin James slipped into a hospital smock and pulled a surgical cap onto his head. The Georgetown medical examiner was already in the police morgue, busy cutting into the corpse of one of the mysterious attackers who had ambushed James, Manning, Takutu and Doraku.

"We authorized the autopsies, but I don't understand why you insisted on this," Barama stated. "The cause of death is obvious. You and Mr. Turner killed these men yourself. I might add, since they murdered Captain Takutu, I'm rather glad you did."

"It would have been better if we'd brought back at least one of 'em alive," James said as he tied a surgical mask around his neck. "Hard to question a dead man. Still, we're gonna try. That's the reason for the autopsies. Sometimes you can learn details about where a man is from and what he's been doing by examining his hands, feet, hair, teeth, digestive system all that stuff."

"I must admit that doesn't make any sense to me," Barama said. "I am a soldier, and this business of forensics is not part of my expertise."

The colonel glanced at the autopsy table. The medical examiner had sliced open a corpse from groin to navel and had pinned back folds of skin with clamps. Barama felt his stomach quiver and looked away.

"Okay," James began. "Dust, soot, ashes and other types of residue can be found on a person's hair, scalp, sometimes in his ears or nostrils. These can give us a good idea where that person spent the last few hours of his life. If he hasn't washed his hair recently, we might even find evidence of where he'd been for more than the last forty-eight hours. Different types of residue can reveal the type of soil in a region, factory smoke, conventional chimneys, that sort of thing. Similar evidence can be found under fingernails, stains on the skin, between toes and so on."

"But why cut the bodies open?" Barama asked, turning slightly toward the autopsy table without actually looking at the procedure again.

"By finding out what sort of food a man has eaten," James explained, "you can get some idea of his lifestyle and where he's come from recently. For example, a lot of seafood in the digestive system would suggest he came from the coast. Certain types of vegetables or tropical fruits are more abundant in some regions than others, and it's more likely people eat large amounts of what's available. We'll also look for traces of alcohol, drugs, stuff like that. Never know what's in there until you go in and look around."

"I see," Barama said with a nod. "I hope you find something useful from all this effort."

"Me too," James confessed as he tied the mask across his nose and mouth. "I've never done so many damn autopsies in such a short period of time as I have since I got here. In the last couple days I've seen more dead people than folks that are still breathing. Corpses don't make very good conversation, you know."

"I imagine they don't," the colonel agreed, eager to get away from the autopsy room. "Good luck, Mr. Brown. I'm going to check with Turner in ballistics now."

Colonel Barama gladly moved to the other lab sections in search of the ballistics department. He stepped around a pair of policemen in the corridor as a door opened to block his path. Emerging from a room, David McCarter raised his eyebrows with surprise when he saw Barama.

"Just the man I was looking for," the Briton declared, and handed the colonel a set of report forms. "Some of your blokes found the truck used by the bastards who attacked our mates out in the jungle. License plates are forgeries. No surprise there. Serial numbers on the engine and other parts suggest the truck had been worked on a bit, with different vehicles cannibalized for parts. The coppers think it was probably stolen or covertly purchased from Venezuela. They're checking into that now. Of course, they're still trying to find out where the two vehicles used by the Haitian and Nepalese mercenaries came from, too, so don't hold your breath waiting to hear from them."

"I see," Barama said lamely. "What should I do with these reports?"

"Don't look at me," McCarter replied. "I gave them to you to get rid of the bloody things. Now I'm gonna look for a Coke machine."

The Briton marched through the hall in his quest for a cold soft drink. Barama tucked the reports under his arm and headed for the ballistics department. He found Gary Manning with a group of technicians. Disassembled firearms were laid across a table. Two ballistics experts examined bullet grooves under microscopes while others copied serial numbers and manufacturer stamps from the weapon parts. Manning looked up at Barama and nodded a mute greeting.

"Hello, Colonel," the Canadian said. "I'm sorry about Captain Takutu. If it's any comfort, he died quickly."

"He was a good soldier," Barama said sadly. "Have you learned anything here?"

"Mostly just confirmed what we already suspected," Manning answered. He gestured at the disassembled firearms. "The men who ambushed us were armed with weapons made in Brazil. Same type of military hardware as the enemy mercenaries had. FAL assault rifles, Beretta M-12 submachine guns and Beretta pistols—all manufactured in Brazil. Technically the subguns are M972s produced by Industria Nacional de Arms SA in São Paulo, but the guns are a licensed copy of the Beretta model. A couple of opponents were armed with Browning PD pistols made in Argentina, but all the ammo was Brazilian."

"But the old shell casings left in the area a year ago were all used to fire blank ammo?" Barama inquired.

"Absolutely, Colonel," one of the technicians replied as he stepped away from a microscope. "Traces of powder in those shell casings were very light, and there were also particles of blank filler at the mouth of each casing. These were also obviously crimped to a far greater degree than would be done with live ammunition. And the shells had been loaded more than once...."

"Thank you," Barama said, trying to cut the man off as politely as possible. He turned his attention to Manning. "Have you any idea how those men managed to track you into the jungle?"

"There was a radio transmitter device planted under the rear bumper of one of our Land Rovers," the Canadian explained. "A receiver unit was found in the enemy's truck."

"Carver gave me these reports on the vehicle, but he didn't mention that," Barama said as he waved the forms.

"Was he in a hurry to find a Coke machine?" Manning inquired.

"Yes," the colonel confirmed. "Do such things slip his mind at such times?"

"Sometimes his priorities get confused," the Phoenix pro said with a shrug. "Anyway, the most important thing we learned from this is the enemy knows enough about us to have planted the bug and to have tried to ambush us. We're obviously causing enough trouble that somebody wants us taken out of action."

"Obviously," Barama agreed. "They must have established an Intelligence network with agents within the military and even the local police here in Georgetown—"

He stopped in midsentence and glanced suspiciously at the lab technicians. They glared back at him, offended by the suggestion they might be traitors. Manning headed for the door, gesturing for Barama to follow.

"It doesn't really matter at this point if the enemy knows a few things about us," the Canadian told him. "If they come after us, it may take us less time to wrap up this mission than if we have to go after them. Still, there are some things we need to discuss privately."

YAKOV KATZ, RAFAEL ENCIZO and CIA case officer Sutcliffe were waiting at the safehouse when Manning and McCarter arrived with Colonel Barama. James was still busy with the autopsies. Sutcliffe held some computer printout forms as he approached the three arrivals.

"Interpol ran a check on Guillotin and Captain Ajmer," he said. "The former Ton Ton Macoute is wanted in Haiti on more than a dozen charges, including murder. A lot of murders, to be exact. Ajmer has a reputation as a totally amoral and apolitical mercenary leader. He's known to have participated in numerous criminal operations in parts of Asia, the Pacific Islands and Africa. No previous operations in this hemisphere, as far as Interpol can tell. They drew a complete blank on Wilkens. Nothing to suggest he's ever broken the law."

"Nothing surprising about that," Katz stated. "We learned something that may help us determine whether or not Wilkens is involved. Some high-ranking members of the People's National Congress are having a fund-raising event at Wellington Hall tonight. Henry Goddard of the Guyanese National Assembly will be there. So will his main supporter, Stanley Wilkens."

"How is this supposed to help us?" Barama asked.

"We need to start surveillance on Wilkens," Katz replied. "You haven't been able to supply us with much manpower. The riots have stopped. We know why, but the police and military still can't spare extra personnel, because they're afraid the violence might flare up again."

"Which will happen unless we find Guillotin, Ajmer and the people who hired them," Encizo added.

"And Wilkens is almost certainly the man responsible," Katz said. He tapped the hooks of the prosthesis on the open palm of his left hand as he spoke. "Trying to plant bugs at his home will be extremely difficult because he lives on a plantation surrounded by more than a hundred acres of sugarcane crops and is no doubt guarded by security devices and armed personnel."

"But he'll be more vulnerable at the fund-raising ball," Encizo stated. "We'll have a chance to rig Wilkens, Goddard, their vehicles and his bodyguard amigos if they show up."

"I don't know if this is a good idea," Barama began.

"I've already tried to talk them out of this," Sutcliffe stated. The Company man sighed and spread his hands in a hopeless gesture. "I've told them that this could be an enormous embarrassment for the United States government if they're wrong. Harassing a member of the Guyanese National Assembly and a leading citizen involved in business—a legal business, as far as we can prove—could make the image of the 'Ugly American' turn absolutely hideous."

"The prime minister isn't going to authorize this," Barama warned them. "I don't even know how to go about asking for permission for something so outrageous."

"Don't tell the prime minister," McCarter suggested. "What he doesn't know about isn't his concern."

"You're asking me to risk my own career," the colonel said with a frown. "That may sound selfish, but my life in the military is very important. Not just for me and my family, but for others of my ethnic background and religion."

"I thought you were a Hindu of Indian descent," Encizo said. "I realize that was an assumption, but I thought it an obvious one."

"I'm of Indian descent," Barama confirmed, "but of Punjabi background. I'm not a Hindu. I happen to be a Sikh. That's a minority religion here in Guyana and one which is not regarded with much favor by any of the major faiths. Sikhism is largely misunderstood by those outside our religion."

"As I recall, Sikhism was founded by Guru Nanak in the fifteenth century," Katz remarked. The Phoenix Force commander was a scholar with a degree in archaeology, and had written three books and numerous articles on the subject. "Nanak's main doctrine was an effort to unify beliefs of the great religions. Didn't he teach that the Godhead was the same regardless of whether it was called Jehovah, Allah, Vishnu or whatever?"

"I am impressed by your knowledge," Barama said with surprise. "You're correct, but I'm sure you also realize Sikhism has been divided in the past and influenced by both Hinduism and Islam in India. Naturally that has made us unpopular with both religions. We're regarded with suspicion and contempt by those who feel we have perverted their religion, or we're perceived as a twisted band of fanatics dedicated to the destruction of other faiths. When Indira Gandhi was assassinated in 1984 by two Sikhs among her own bodyguards, it rekindled all the prejudice we've had to deal with in the past."

"I take it there aren't very many Sikhs among the field-grade officers in the military in Guyana," McCarter commented.

"That's right," Barama said with a nod. "I'm something of a spokesman or representative of the Punjabi and Sikh community here. If I'm involved in a national scandal, it will unfairly reflect on all my people. Do you understand?"

"Yes, we understand," Katz assured him. "We don't want to cause any problems for you or add to any woes of Sikhs in Guyana. Nonetheless we have a mission to carry out and we're in charge right now. All you have to do is get us the surveillance gear we'll need and some trustworthy personnel to help monitor it. The responsibility will be ours.''

"And the CIA will suffer for any mistakes you make,'' Sutcliffe muttered. ''I know you guys have White House authority and you outrank me, but I'm still concerned about the reputation of the Company.''

"I hate to break this news to you,'' Encizo said dryly, "but the CIA's reputation went down the tubes almost twenty years ago.''

"If that's true, it's because the Company meddled in the affairs of foreign nations,'' Sutcliffe replied angrily. "People like you were responsible for that, but you never seem to learn from past mistakes.''

"I'm not going to waste time defending what we do,'' Katz said quickly before McCarter or Encizo could respond with sharp-tongued remarks—or possibly worse. "We're not responsible for any blunders or embarrassments associated with the CIA, past or present. You may question whether what we do is right or not, but we don't have any doubts about it.''

"If we're correct about Wilkens being involved in a scheme to take over Guyana,'' Manning began, "that's something that should alarm everyone in both South and North America. Haven't there been enough rotten dictatorships in the western hemisphere? If this really is an attempt by organized forces from Nazi strongholds in South America to seize control of the country, it won't stop here any more than Hitler intended to stop after he invaded Poland.''

"I still find that Nazi theory hard to believe,'' the CIA man insisted.

At that moment Calvin James entered the safehouse, approached the Company man and handed him a manila envelope.

"Then maybe you ought to be the first to see these, smartass," James declared, and wearily headed for the coffee maker.

Sutcliffe opened the envelope and removed several photographs and handwritten reports. He frowned as he noticed some of the photos were blowup shots of men's hairy armpits. The CIA case officer thought these pictures were disgusting and failed to realize the importance until he noticed each armpit had different numbers tattooed on the skin.

"These are obviously some kind of identification marks," Sutcliffe stated. "I heard the Nazi SS officers used to have similar tattoos under their arms."

Katz leaned forward to examine one of the photos. His facial muscles tensed, and his mouth formed a tight hard line. Katz's normally gentle blue eyes seemed to burn with rage, yet suddenly revealed sadness. He closed his eyes for a brief moment and took a deep breath, and the wave of emotion seemed to have passed when he opened them again. The fellow Phoenix Force commandos knew their unit leader could not switch his feelings off and on at will, but he had the mental discipline and concentration to avoid having emotions muddle his judgement.

"These are exactly like the SS identification tattoos," he announced. "Believe me, I have good reason to remember what they look like."

"You'll also notice there are photographs of other tattoos," James declared. "Swastikas and SS rune markings are tattooed on shoulders and under arms. Places that wouldn't be obvious when a person is wearing as little as an undershirt. You still think there's no evidence of a Nazi involvement or at least a neo-Nazi outfit behind this mess, Sutcliffe?"

"Well, this is the first hard evidence we've come up with," Manning added, giving the CIA man a chance to save face.

"And I'd say it's enough for us to concentrate on your proposal to conduct surveillance on Wilkens," Sutcliffe said with a firm nod. "I just hope we're not barking up the wrong tree. Your suspicions are based on very circumstantial evidence."

"That's why we're going to try to get something of more substance tonight," Katz assured him. "Unfortunately that means we have very little time to get ready for the ball."

"You'll have everything you need," Barama vowed. "I'm ashamed I even considered putting my career before the well-being of my country. As for being a role model for other Sikhs or representing them in any way, I doubt I'd do my people justice if I turned my back and looked away from evil instead of trying to fight it."

"That's a fight that will always exist," Katz remarked.

13

The gray limousine drove past the Saint George Cathedral, the beautiful and majestic white church in the heart of Georgetown. Constructed almost entirely of wood, the cathedral is one of the largest and best-known buildings in the capital. Otto Weissflog had seen it many times before and barely glanced at it. He had little regard for Catholicism, but at least it was a Christian faith. With enough government controls of the clergy, Catholicism would be allowed to continue after he seized power in Guyana.

Weissflog noticed two men dressed in work coveralls by a telephone repair truck across the street. They were brown-skinned figures with turbans wrapped around their heads, he observed with contempt. Weissflog had vowed that the Hindu pagans and other non-Christian religions would have to be stomped out. They were too foreign to the beliefs of the white Aryan "master race" and would not fit into the society he planned for the future.

Rafael Encizo, dressed in work clothes and a turban, watched the limo pass as he stood behind the telephone truck. The Cuban's dark complexion allowed him to pass for an Indian in the shadows of night. He braced a leather-bound toolbox by his thigh and pointed it at the limo. Encizo judged the distance and triggered the firing mechanism in the handle. A powerful CO_2 cartridge ejected a steel dart from the barrel of a device built into the toolbox.

The dart struck the big gray automobile just below the trunk. Pleased with his aim, Encizo watched the limo continue along the street. His companion, a Guyana Defense Forces communicatons expert named Biloku, looked at Encizo and nodded.

"Very good marksmanship, sir," Biloku declared. "That device is difficult to fire accurately. That is most impressive for a first shot."

"It's similar to a variation of a skindiver's speargun," Encizo replied. "I've had a lot of experience with those. Let's see if the transmitter is working."

They climbed into the telephone truck, which was really a surveillance rig in disguise. It was equipped with a periscope with a long-range infrared lens, radio receivers, a rifle microphone and a tracking screen similar to that used for radar. Biloku switched on a radio to an infinity receiver unit. Voices spoke in German, a language neither Encizo nor Biloku understood fluently. The communications man turned on a tape recorder.

"One of your friends will have to translate this later," Biloku remarked. "Now, the transmitter has a range of almost two kilometers. Metal and glass pick up vibrations. Sound has vibrations, of course. The engine and spinning tires will distort the reception, but we should be able to get most of their conversation as long as they don't have any scrambling devices or the dart works free from the metal skin of the automobile."

"Good work, Biloku," Encizo said. He had used similar surveillance equipment in the past, but realized the commo expert enjoyed displaying his expertise for a stranger. "Okay, we'll have to tail them, but we have to take care not to get too close."

He listened to the voices on the machine. Two or more males and one woman, Encizo noticed. Wilkens had brought his wife and no doubt his bodyguards. His son might be in the limo, as well. The Phoenix commando pulled the turban from his head and started to remove the coveralls. He wore a black outfit under the work clothes.

"I'll drive," he announced. "You watch the equipment and let me know if we start losing them."

The telephone truck pursued the limousine at a distance. Encizo drove the rig and switched on a two-way radio in the front seat to contact the other members of Phoenix Force. He informed them that they had successfully bugged Wilkens's car and the plantation owner was conversing in German with the others in the vehicle.

"Interesting that a British Guyanese would choose to chat with his chums in a language other than English," McCarter's voice replied from the radio.

"Maybe he's taking a Berlitz course and he's practicing German with the other passengers," Encizo fatuously suggested. "Better stay alert, because they're headed your way."

"We're ready for 'em," the Briton assured his partner.

"I sure hope so," Encizo said. "Over and out."

The Cuban set the radio on the seat beside him and returned his right hand to the steering wheel. The traffic was light, and Encizo had no trouble following the limousine. His biggest challenge was to remain inconspicuous. The Phoenix pro let a public transportation bus and several cars pull in between the surveillance rig and the limo.

"Two kilometers," Encizo thought out loud as he recalled the range of the transmitter. "Hey, Biloku! Are you still getting good reception on the receiver back there?"

"A lot of noise from the limo itself, but no other problems," the Guyanese called back to Encizo. "Static is minimum, and the voices aren't faded."

"Good," the Cuban declared as he glanced over a street map of Georgetown. "I don't want to be close enough for them to see us. I'll pull onto another street and approach Wellington Hall from a different direction. Let me know if we start to lose them on the radio."

Encizo steered the truck onto Churchill Street and headed west. Georgetown was structured in a manner similar to many capital cites, including Washington, DC, with some streets forming circles and others crossing them in a spiderweb pattern. The Cuban thought this design was appropriate, because he had a cynical attitude toward politicians. He believed government was a necessary evil, but some forms are more desirable than others. In his own country he had suffered the most from Communism, so that form was at the head of his hate list. Fascism came in a close second.

If Wilkens was trying to establish a Nazi regime in Guyana, Encizo figured the son of a bitch had to be stopped. He didn't know much about the present government in Guyana. Although Guyana was technically a socialist country, it was heavily influenced by long traditions of British common law. Whatever else could be said about Guyana, it had not invaded its neighbors or tried to force its system of government on other countries. This would certainly change if the fanatics of National Socialism gained control.

The best way to handle cancer is to cut out the malignant growth as soon as possible, Encizo thought as he drove the truck along Churchill Street. All the shops and markets were closed, and the street lighting was poor. The Cuban felt as if he was rolling through a big dark alley. Instinctively he patted the Walther P-88 under his left arm and found comfort in the knowledge it was loaded.

A pair of headlights appeared in the rearview mirror. The only other vehicle on the quiet, dark street was closing in fast. Encizo heard the roar of the other engine and recognized the outline of a dark sedan in the shadows. He resisted the urge to stomp on the gas, aware the lighter car could certainly outrace the heavier telephone repair vehicle.

"¡Madre de Dios!" he rasped as the sedan shot alongside the truck.

Encizo looked out the window and saw two men in the front seat of the sedan. He couldn't see whether there were more in the backseat. The two in the front appeared to be East Indians or, more likely, Nepalese mercs. One leaned out the open window on the passenger's side and pointed a Beretta M-12 submachine gun at the truck. The Cuban instantly turned the wheel hard and stomped on the gas.

The larger vehicle swerved and crashed into the sedan. Metal scraped metal, and sparks spat up from the violent friction. The unexpected impact sent the car skidding out of control. Encizo heard a scream of agony and saw the arms of the would-be gunman dangle useless and broken from the car window. The sedan slid across the street and crashed into the storefront window of a fish market. Glass shattered as the car plunged through the window like a deranged rhino.

Encizo pulled onto the sidewalk ten yards from the other vehicle and braked. When the truck screeched to a halt, Encizo popped open the door and jumped out, Walther pistol already in his fist. The Cuban jogged to the crippled sedan. A dazed and frightened Biloku opened the back of the rig and stared at the rear end of the car that jutted from the shattered store window.

A rear door of the sedan opened, and a Nepalese gunman emerged with a stainless-steel revolver in his fist. Shaken and disoriented, the man failed to take aim fast enough. Encizo already had the Walther trained on the mercenary's chest. The Cuban triggered two shots. Orange flame leaped from the muzzle of his P-88, and the gunman fell back against the sedan and collapsed lifeless on the pavement.

Encizo moved behind the vehicle, Walther held ready in a Weaver's combat grip. Using the car for cover, he peered around it carefully. No one was visible through the windows of the sedan. The driver's door was open. The Cuban sucked in a tense breath and started to climb through the smashed store window.

Someone lunged from the shadows within the shop. Encizo glimpsed a heavy steel blade as it slashed at his hands and wrists. He drew back, but the thick crescent of steel struck the Walther and sent it hurtling. His opponent charged forward. A stocky, well-muscled man with a fierce dark face, the merc swung his *kukri* knife in a backhand stroke aimed at the Cuban's head and neck.

Encizo ducked under the deadly slash. The *kukri* whirled above his head. Encizo slammed his forearm into the attacker's wrist, above the thick curved blade. With his other hand he drew the Cold Steel Tanto from its belt sheath and delivered a fast, upward slash. The mercenary shrieked as the blade sliced into his armpit. The *kukri* fell from his fingers and clattered to the floor.

The man's other hand clawed for Encizo's face and eyes. The Cuban moved away from the gouging fingers and thrust the slanted tip of the Tanto under the merc's chin. The Cold Steel blade pierced the hollow of the goon's throat. Blood spewed from the man's open mouth as he staggered backward and clawed at the lethal wound, eyes wide with the astonishment of meeting sudden death. His knees buckled, and he wilted to the pavement as the last remnants of life spilled from his punctured throat.

"Good Lord!" Biloku exclaimed as he approached the Cuban, staring at the carnage with disbelief. "What happened?"

"Someone noticed we were following Wilkens's limo and they tried to ambush us," Encizo explained. "A carload of Ajmer's soldiers for hire. Damn it, I should have thought something like this might happen. Wilkens suspects we're onto him. It would make sense to have another vehicle watch for anyone tailing him."

"Does that mean he knows about the transmitter?" Biloku asked. "I'll check the car to see if they have a radio transceiver."

"Loan me your side arm and I'll check it," Encizo declared. "There's another goon inside. I don't think he's in any shape to cause trouble, but I don't want to take any chances."

Biloku obediently handed Encizo his .38 S&W revolver.

"Now, head back to the truck," Encizo instructed as he glanced about the deserted street, glad there were no witnesses or pedestrians. "Radio our friends and tell them we're going to be a few minutes late to the ball."

14

Wellington Hall was a large handsome building of imported white marble with Doric-style columns and stained-glass windows. Several limousines and Mercedes Sedans had already arrived at the hall when Weissflog's car rolled up the pebbled driveway. Calvin James watched from the door of the hall as the limo pulled up. Werner emerged from the front passenger seat to open the door for Stanley Wilkens and his wife.

Dressed in a black tuxedo, with a black bowler derby perched on his sleek head, the plantation owner looked dignified and debonair. Karin wore a white evening gown with long white gloves and a minimum of jewelry. There was nothing sinister in their appearance. The couple could have belonged to the Royal Family.

James hoped he didn't look as awkward as he felt, dressed in a formal dinner jacket, frilled silk shirt and black tie. He was accustomed to wearing camouflage fatigues and conventional street clothes. Formal attire felt like a costume. Of course, James was pretending to be someone he was not, and the dinner jacket was part of his disguise. For him, the ball was a serious and potentially dangerous masquerade.

He recognized Wilkens from photographs and descriptions. The two bodyguards left no room for doubt. They looked like a pro wrestling tag team dressed in tuxedos. A valet parked the limo while the two Nordic hulks followed their boss up the steps. James moved away from the door and nearly backed into Yakov Katz.

"Wilkens is here," James whispered.

Katz nodded. The Israeli didn't look odd in a tux, James noticed. Katz could easily pass for a successful banker, businessman or even a judge. He seemed relaxed and comfortable in the starched collar and black tie—the same outfit that threatened to throttle James. Katz held a glass of white wine and raised it to his lips without taking a sip. He wore pearl-gray gloves. One concealed a steel five-fingers prosthesis that was less obvious than the trident hooks of his usual artificial limb. It was less functional than the hooks, but his right "hand" appeared to be one of flesh and muscle, except to an astute observer who might notice that the fingers were rigid. Actually the artificial index finger was immobile, but the other three digits and the synthetic thumb could perform limited manipulations in a pincerlike fashion.

"We need to talk," Katz told James, and strolled across the ballroom.

An orchestra performed a Mozart symphony and a few couples were waltzing. Katz, who knew the music well, was rather amused, aware that the tempo of the music was deceptively simple in the beginning, but would soon pick up enough to throw the dancers off guard.

The ballroom was vast, featuring an ornate marble floor. The buffet table, with an assortment of fine dishes and drinks, was nearly twenty feet long. Most of the guests were clustered in groups, busy with conversation. The largest of these was the congregation of People's National Assembly party members who were trying to get the ear of the prime minister of Guyana, the highest-ranking government official to attend the event.

Katz and James shuffled through the crowd and found Colonel Barama and George Sutcliffe in a corner. The colonel wore a formal dress uniform, medals and ribbons on his chest. The CIA man resembled an overweight penguin in his ill-fitting tuxedo.

"Biloku called in with a disturbing report," Katz told James as he turned to keep watch on Weissflog and his companions from a distance. "The phone truck was ambushed."

"Is Raf... Mr. Gonzales okay?" James asked tensely.

"He's fine," Katz assured his partner. "But this means Wilkens may suspect we're watching him."

"Hell, he got suspicious of two of our guys, and he probably figures we're suspicious of him, too," James said. "Wilkens's goons didn't remove the transmitter dart from the limo when they arrived. The valet who parked the car is one of your men, isn't he, Colonel?"

"Yes," Barama confirmed. "He'll remove the dark and plant some less obvious button microphones in the vehicle. He's a very reliable man, experienced with this sort of work. Biloku tells me this fellow worked with him before on surveillance operations of individuals suspected of being members of a Communist extremist group and loyal to former Guyanese prime minster Cheddi Jagan. Turned out that alleged conspiracy was a total fabrication."

"The one we have on our hands now isn't," Katz reminded him. The Israeli noticed a slim, middle-aged man with wavy gray hair heading toward Wilkens's group. "Is that Goddard?"

The man in question, one of the few whites present, moved with easy confidence, obviously accustomed to being in a position of authority. The man's lush gray hair appeared to be professionally styled, and he displayed beautifully capped white teeth as he smiled and nodded politely. His assured manner was reminiscent of British stage actors who have already achieved knighthood and have good reason to believe the Queen will soon award them lordship, as well.

"That's right," Barama told Katz. "Henry Goddard, honored member of the National Assembly and long-time friend of Mr. Stanley Wilkens."

"Let's go introduce ourselves," Katz announced. "You will be subtle, Mr. Brown?"

"Shee-it, man," James replied with an exaggerated street jive. "I be cool."

Katz and James crossed the room and slipped between the well-dressed guests. Although this was a fund-raiser for the PNC, many diplomats from embassies had been invited and a smattering of representatives from Trinidad, Brazil and Venezuela were present. It was an international assembly, but most of the conversations were in English.

Weissflog and Goddard spoke quietly, heads bowed close together. Werner and Reinhard, glancing about like a pair of hawks, stiffened as Gary Manning approached. Neither bodyguard noticed Katz and James until the Phoenix pair stepped next to Goddard.

"I beg your pardon, gentlemen," Katz began, effecting a realistic British accent with a Cambridge flavor. "I don't want to interrupt anything, but I do need to ask a question or two."

"What?" Goddard asked, startled by being accosted by the stranger. "Just a moment, please . . ."

"A moment is all the time we need," Katz assured him. "I'm Huntington-Smythe. This is my associate, Mr. Davies."

"Delighted to meet you," James announced with a convincing Jamaican accent, speaking in an almost musical manner. "I've heard a great deal about you, Mr. Goddard."

He clasped Goddard's hand, shook it with enthusiasm. James's left hand gripped the politician's forearm to reinforce the generous pumping of the handshake. The black commando smiled broadly and bobbed his head to further distract Goddard. The Guyanese didn't notice James had pinned a small black button to his sleeve. No bigger than a match head, the button was virtually invisible pinned to the black fabric of Goddard's tux.

"You see, we're with a British-owned company with branches in the Commonwealth nations," Katz stated. He didn't attempt to shake hands with Goddard, not wishing to draw attention to his prosthesis. After James's overzealous behavior, no one noticed. "Our branch headquarters is in Jamaica."

"Really?" Goddard replied, annoyed by the conversation and eager to get rid of the pair.

Manning approached the group. He smiled at Weissflog as if pleased to see an old friend. Karin returned the gesture with a polite nod, but Weissflog simply glared at Manning. The bodyguards glanced at their boss, waiting for a signal to tell them whether they should stand by quietly or haul Manning out of the ballroom.

"Hello, Mr. Wilkens," Manning greeted. "I wondered if you'd be here."

"I was invited," Weissflog replied. "I hadn't expected to see you here. You Canadian journalists must make friends quickly. I suppose men in your profession have connections with people in high places.''

"And sometimes we meet low people in high places," Manning told him.

Calvin James placed a hand on Weissflog's shoulder. The Nazi shivered, disgusted that a black man had touched him. James smiled and surreptitiously pinned a black button to Weissflog's tuxedo.

"I say," James began. "Mr. Wilkens? Right? You wouldn't happen to be involved in the lumber business?"

"No," Weissflog snarled through his teeth, glaring at the black man. "I run a sugar plantation."

"Oh?" James said as he bobbed his head. "That's too bad. Not for you, of course, but we're trying to get some lumber trade established with Guyana. Jamaica has its own sugar crops, you know. My company needs more imported hardwoods for furniture and other wood products."

"I'm afraid I can't help you," Weissflog said dryly.

"And I must insist that we discuss this matter at another time," Goddard told Katz. The Israeli had babbled about the fictional needs of his company to the politician while Manning spoke with Weissflog. "Call my office and make an appointment to meet me first of next week."

"But we're going back to Jamaica in three days," Katz said with a frown. "You're sure you can't arrange anything sooner? I mean, you are more *British* than most of these Guyanese we've had to deal with."

"If you think I'm going to be more receptive to your requests because I'm white," Goddard began in a weary voice, "I'm afraid you are sadly mistaken. The minister of forestry and land resources is here somewhere. I suggest you talk to him.''

''Very well,'' Katz said with a sigh. ''Thank you for your time.''

''Sorry if we were a bother for you gents,'' James added as he backed away from Goddard and displayed a massive shrug.

Katz and James headed across the ballroom. Weissflog returned his attention to Gary Manning. The Canadian's poker-faced expression revealed nothing of his thoughts. Weissflog fixed an icy gaze on Manning's eyes and smiled without mirth.

''You and Carver rejected my gift of dinner the other night,'' he stated. ''That was rather insulting of you.''

''Maybe that was the reason we did it,'' Manning replied. ''How's the sugar business these days? I understand you've had a couple big setbacks recently.''

''That happens from time to time,'' the Nazi said with a slight shrug. ''There's always a way to deal with problems if you have enough determination.''

''Oh, yeah,'' Manning agreed. ''We're pretty good at handling problems, too. Did you know I caught a couple guys in my room at the hotel?''

''Thieves?'' Weissflog inquired with feined ignorance.

''I didn't ask them,'' the Canadian replied. ''The police have them now, so I guess they won't be any trouble to anyone else. Terrible about all this violence that's suddenly occurred in Guyana. You figure it will come to an end soon?''

''You may not be around long enough to know how it turns out, Mr. Turner,'' the Nazi told him.

''Don't count on it,'' Manning said. ''I'm not leaving the country until I've finished my job here.''

"Then be careful," Weissflog advised with a frosty smile. "The job might finish you first."

Goddard didn't like the way their conversation was headed. He cleared his throat loudly to get Weissflog's attention.

"Yes, Henry," Weissflog said with a nod. "Excuse us, Mr. Turner. I have other business to discuss."

"I'll see you later," Manning assured him, and walked away.

The Canadian resisted the urge to glance over his shoulder to see whether Werner and Reinhard were following him. David McCarter was watching the ballroom from an adjacent room. Manning trusted the Briton to watch his back. He was also confident Stanley Wilkens would not be foolish enough to approve of strong-arm tactics in front of so many witnesses, but he was not as sure of the intelligence of the two bodyguards. The stupid bastards might try to nail him before their owner could call them off.

Manning stepped behind a group of guests gathered around the prime minster. He used the cluster of humanity to cover his actions as he peered between them to watch Weissflog and Goddard. The pair were headed for the front door, followed by Karin and the bodyguards. Colonel Barama appeared next to Manning.

"Your friends have found an interesting channel on their radio," the officer whispered. "And another friend has arrived with some tape recordings you may want to hear."

"Good," Manning replied. "I'm too close to these politicians and I'm afraid I'll be bored to death if I have to listen to them exchange lies to one another."

"How do you know they're lying?" Barama asked.

"Their lips move," the Canadian replied, and moved across the room as quickly as possible without drawing attention to himself.

RAFAEL ENCIZO AND BILOKU had arrived at the professional kitchen at Wellington Hall. Two of Barama's men met them at the door and assured the cooking staff the pair were supposed to be there. The Cuban and the Guyanese communications expert entered the kitchen and followed one of the soldiers through a corridor to the office of the assistant curator. Katz and Sutcliffe, sitting at a desk in the room, looked up as Encizo and Biloku entered.

"Glad you could make it," Katz declared. "I understand you had some car trouble."

"You might say that," Encizo replied as he pulled a *kukri* knife from his belt. "One of the ambushers had one of these."

Sutcliffe's eyes widened. The twelve-inch blade extended from a buffalo-horn handle and curved into a heavy chopping instrument. The sharp edge was at the inside of the curve. The *kukri* was an ideal weapon for decapitation.

"That's a wicked-looking thing," the CIA man remarked.

"It looked a lot more wicked when it was in the hands of a man who was trying to kill me," Encizo told him.

The Cuban tried to place the *kukri* on the desk, but there was little room available. A radio transmitter with a tape recorder attached, as well as two Uzi machine pistols, sat on the desktop. Voices spoke from the speaker of the machine.

"We managed to plant button microphones on Wilkens and Goddard," Katz said. "They seem to be having a private conversation outside."

He turned up the volume. The voices became louder. Katz adjusted the static knob to get clearer reception and checked the tape machine to be certain it was recording.

"Otto, you're rushing everything," Goddard's voice declared. "Those damn niggers from Haiti and the Gurkha wogs you hired have made a bloody mess of this whole operation. I warned you that this wasn't the time for it. Not after killing that Yank senator's son. There's too much attention on Guyana now."

"Don't you believe in destiny?" Weissflog's voice inquired. "No, you're only half German, so your faith isn't strong enough. The incident at the village was an omen. We were being told by God Himself that it was time to stop training and preparing, and take direct action."

"Crazy bastard," Sutcliffe whispered as he listened to the conversation. He glanced up at Katz. "Looks like you guys were right."

Katz held a finger to his lips to urge the Company man to be quiet and listen.

"A message from God?" Goddard's voice said with a groan. "You think they'll listen to that if we stand trial for treason?"

"Treason against the state?" Weissflog's voice replied. "That is nothing compared to *Landesverrat*. You and I are *Volksgenosse*. It is our sacred duty to continue in our struggle to establish a true Germanic democracy in this country and eventually throughout the world."

"I don't understand what he's talking about," Sutcliffe admitted.

"The term *Landesverrat* means 'treason against the fatherland' and was regarded as the most grievous crime by the Nazis in Germany,'' Katz explained. "*Volksgenosse* means 'racial comrades.' Apparently Wilkens regards Goddard as good Aryan stock, equal to himself from a racial point of view."

"And a 'Germanic democracy'?" the CIA man asked.

"Hitler spoke of it in *Mein Kampf*," the Phoenix commander answered, wishing Sutcliffe would wait until the conversation between the two conspirators was over before he asked such questions. "Supposedly the Nazi concept of a 'Germanic democracy' is one that puts a great leader and a hero in command of a nation, giving him absolute authority. He's supposed to accept absolute responsibility in return. In other words, it's not anything like a true democracy."

The voices on the tape continued. Goddard was speaking. "You know I believe in our cause, but too much has gone wrong the last two or three days. Even I can't learn any details about these strangers who are working with the Defense Forces. Security is that tight."

"That man Turner is one of them," Weissflog stated. "Damn traitor to his own race. I'll give him credit for arrogance. It took a bold man to walk up to me and speak as he did tonight."

"You should have killed him when you had the chance," Goddard said grimly.

"I only suspected he and Carver might be CIA or British Intelligence or whatever," Weissflog replied. "That's why I told Guillotin to search their rooms at the hotel. The black apes he sent botched the job. Turner and Carver haven't returned to the Royal Inn since. My men tried to take Turner out in the jungle, but these men are no ordinary warriors. Killing them won't be easy."

"Maybe the killing should stop for a while," Goddard advised.

Gary Manning entered the office and joined the others at the desk. He remained silent and listened to the voices from the radio.

"I don't like doing this," Weissflog stated. "Taking these lives has been repugnant to me. Even if most of those killed are racial inferiors, unfit to run this country, I would not be part of these killings unless it was necessary to cleanse Guyana and establish a righteous rule with white masters in charge. Having blacks and Indians running a country is a 'monster of excrement and flames,' as *der Fuhrer* would say."

"Your *Fuhrer* isn't here," Goddard declared. "And Guyana isn't Germany in 1933. Even if your plan succeeds and both the president and the prime minster die, that doesn't put me in charge of the country."

"Look at how easy it has been to get the Indians and the blacks to turn against one another," Weissflog insisted. "That same distrust and hatred they feel for each other caused riots in the early 1960s, which resulted in the British troops coming in to restore order. Britain is no longer a world power. Guyana can't turn to them again. They'll have to turn to the *white* racially superior members of their own nation to save them from themselves. The blacks and Indians are inferiors and they have to be treated as little children with white masters in charge to protect and guide them. Still, they are not basically evil or corrupt like *ein Judlein*."

"German equivalent of 'Jew-kike,'" Katz translated before Sutcliffe could ask what the last term meant.

"So, have faith and be strong, Henry," Weissflog urged. "Don't worry about our enemies. They will be taken care of. Most of all, don't enter the dining room tonight when they announce dinner."

Sutcliffe frowned. "Why did he say that?"

"They were talking about killing the president and the prime minister," Katz replied as he stood and reached for one of the Uzis. "Tonight is as good a time as any to get the prime minister. In fact this fund-raiser presents an opportunity to remove a number of high-ranking officials who could stand in Goddard's way from taking control of the country after the present leaders are gone."

"When's dinner scheduled?" Encizo asked.

"Eight-thirty," Manning answered, checking his watch. "That's less than two minutes from now."

15

"What are you going to do?" Sutcliffe asked fearfully as Manning grabbed an Uzi machine pistol from the desk.

"What the hell do you think?" Encizo replied gruffly. The Cuban took a canvas knapsack from his shoulder. He unzipped it to extract his Uzi and three spare 32-round magazines. "One for each of us."

"Thank you," Katz said, and accepted an extra mag, shoving it in the waistband of his tuxedo pants.

"You can't just charge into the dining room with those guns..." Sutcliffe began, his voice strained and nearly breaking.

"This is no time to worry about appearances," Manning growled as he took the other spare Uzi magazine. "You think we'll offend some Guyanese politicians? Jesus, fella! Somebody's ready to offend a bunch of them to death!"

The three Phoenix commandos charged into the corridor, followed by Biloku. The Guyanese commo man asked what he should do. Calvin James appeared at the end of the hall and stared at the Uzis with surprise.

"What's going down?" he asked.

"Just follow us," Katz answered. "We'll fill you in. Is Carver still at his post?"

"As far as I know," James replied. "Don't I get an Uzi?"

"You broke yours," Manning told him.

"I didn't break it," James muttered. "It was shot outta my hands, if you recall. Bolt was damaged. Didn't we pack a spare?"

"We didn't bring it this trip," Encizo said. He glanced over his shoulder at Biloku. "Best thing for you to do is go back in the office and monitor the equipment. Protect those tapes with your life. That's our proof about Wilkens and Goddard. I don't trust Sutcliffe to look after it on his own."

"Yes, sir," Biloku said, and headed back to the office.

He bumped into Sutcliffe at the doorway. The CIA man pushed past him and jogged through the corridor after the Phoenix commandos. They marched steadily toward the ballroom, unconcerned with Sutcliffe's complaints that they were charging in without thinking.

"Find Barama," Katz ordered, not bothering to turn to look at the Company agent. "Tell him to have his men cover all exits outside the hall. If they find Wilkens out there, place him under arrest."

They continued toward the ballroom. Two servants, dressed in red jackets and black trousers, saw the Phoenix Force warriors approach. The sight startled the young black waiters. Two of the guests carried compact machine pistols with shoulder straps, weapons poised at hip level. Another guest didn't have a gun in view, but his stern expression warned that he was a willing accomplice with the others. The fourth figure was the most formidable in appearance. Encizo still wore black cammies, and his Walther pistol in shoulder leather and Tanto knife in a belt sheath were as visible as his Uzi.

The servants retreated into the ballroom. All four Phoenix veterans noticed the waiters seemed more surprised than frightened. Neither man cried out in fear, and both seemed almost angry when they spotted the commandos. Their retreat did not appear panic-stricken or even nervous.

"Shit," James rasped. "Barama has some of his men among the hired help. We should have figured Wilkens might do the same."

"We didn't completely overlook the possibility," Katz reminded him.

David McCarter was posted in a room adjacent to the ballroom to watch the guests in general and the prime minister in particular. Phoenix Force had guessed any plan for a takeover in Guyana would include assassinating the current leaders, but they had not expected Wilkens to be bold enough to carry out multiple assassinations at the hall.

"We overlooked more than we should have," Manning said grimly as they marched into the ballroom.

MOST OF THE VIP GUESTS TURNED to the entrance of the dining room as a tall Indian servant, clad in a handsome gold jacket with a high collar and a light blue turban, announced dinner was ready. Some guests saw the four Phoenix commandos. They gasped with astonishment and backed away in terror, eyes fixed on the weapons in the strangers' hands.

The warriors ignored the startled expressions of the crowd. Katz and Manning marched to the center of the ballroom. James and Encizo concentrated on watching the servants. One of the waiters headed for the great marble staircase and started to ascend the stone risers. James spotted the guy and turned in pursuit.

Manning glanced up at the three marble balconies above the ballroom. Each was ideally located for an ambush as a secondary plan of action in case the enemy's original scheme to assassinate the guests at dinner failed. Had Wilkens considered this? Manning figured they could not afford to ignore any possibility when dealing with a cunning madman such as the Nazi leader.

"Freeze, asshole!" James shouted. He had removed his Walther P-88 from inside his jacket and trained it at the waiter on the stairs.

The man stopped abruptly and slowly raised his hands. James gestured for the waiter to move back down the stairs. Alarmed voices sounded throughout the ballroom.

Katz swung his Uzi toward the man in the gold jacket by the dining room. He addressed the crowd in a loud, commanding voice: "Everyone stay where you are! Try to stay calm. Mr. Prime Minister?"

Katz kept his Uzi trained on the Indian servant by the dining room as he spoke to the highest-ranking government official in the room. The prime minister stepped forward. His wife clutched his arm and tried to restrain him, but he patted her hand and assured her everything would be all right. He wished he believed his own words.

"What do you want?" the prime minister asked Katz. He was an astute man, accustomed to observing situations before making judgments. The politician noticed none of the armed men in the ballroom threatened him or any other government representative. "What is this about?"

"We've uncovered a plot to assassinate you, sir," Katz announced. "A plot to overthrow your government and establish a fanatical new regime that would endanger all nations in this hemisphere."

"He's telling the truth, sir," Colonel Barama declared as he approached with Sutcliffe at his heels. "We have proof of this conspiracy."

He thrust an accusing finger at Henry Goddard. The corrupt politician seemed stunned as his eyes expanded in his pale face and he began to tremble with terror.

"And that man is part of it!" Barama announced.

The crowd buzzed with astonishment and disbelief. James shoved the waiter into a wall and forced him to adopt a spread-eagled stance. The American jammed the muzzle of his P-88 into the guy's ribs and frisked him. He found a compact .380 Astra Constable autoloader at the small of the man's back. James confiscated the pistol and stuck it in his belt.

"How many others?" he demanded. Aware the guy was probably a Haitian, James repeated the question in French.

"Je ne comprends pas," the waiter replied.

"You'd better friggin' understand," James growled, and dug the Walther barrel painfully under the Haitian's ribs. *"Combien?"*

Gunshots erupted outside the building. The reports of automatic weapons and pistols indicated Barama's soldiers had encountered enemy forces. People screamed and shouted and scrambled about in panic. To their credit, the prime minster, his wife and a few assembly members and diplomats tried to urge everyone to calm down. Unfortunately the majority bolted in blind terror for the nearest exits. Driven by unreasoning fear, they failed to realize they were heading toward instead of away from the shooting.

"Stupid bastards," Katz rasped with disgust as several figures ran between his Uzi and the guy he had been covering with the gun.

The man in the gold jacket retreated into the dining room, confident Katz would not risk shooting innocent bystanders. Encizo aimed his Uzi high and blasted a short salvo into the plaster above the front door. Bullet holes formed a line across the arch, and plaster dust showered down on terrified guests. The abrupt warning effectively drove them back, away from the door.

"Get down and stay away from the windows and doors!" the Cuban ordered. "They're not setting off fireworks outside!"

THE HAITIAN WAITER, figuring the shooting would distract James, whirled and swung his forearm at James's gun hand. James jerked away from the Haitian's attack and instantly delivered a snap-kick to the thug's abdomen. The phony servant gasped and started to double-over from the kick. James whipped the barrel of his Walther across the goon's jaw. The Haitian fell to his hands and knees. The Phoenix warrior chopped the butt of his P-88 behind his opponent's right ear. The man sprawled unconscious at James's feet.

"Oh, shit," the American rasped when he glanced up the staircase and saw two armed figures on the landing.

A pair of Nepalese mercenaries dressed in night camouflage uniforms pointed their Beretta M-12 choppers at the Phoenix pro. James jumped behind one of the two marble posts, at the foot of the stairs. The enemy submachine guns blasted 9 mm slugs that sparked on stone and whined past. Bullets chewed a line of bloodied holes between the shoulder blades of the unconscious Haitian.

James slipped the barrel of his P-88 across the Y-shaped junction where the handrail met the marble post. He couldn't aim properly without exposing his head to enemy fire. The Nepalese gunmen were in an elevated position and armed with full-auto weapons. The situation was hardly one James would have chosen, but he had to handle the circumstances as best he could.

He triggered three shots at the mercs, hoping to force the pair to duck or to disorient them a bit. He was not optimistic enough to think he might hit one of the bastards. The hardass from Chicago pulled the confiscated Astra pistol from his belt with his free hand and peered around the post. The merc killers had ducked. James pointed the .380 Constable at one of them and fired blindly with the 9 mm Walther.

The P-88 rounds urged the enemy to stay low. James triggered the Astra as fast as the mechanism allowed. The compact Constable was a double-action autoloader, similar in design to the famous Walther PPK. It barked three times. An enemy mercenary jerked violently from the impact of .380 slugs to his upper torso. James shifted the aim of the Constable and fired two shots at the second merc. The thug retreated across the landing, apparently unharmed.

The wounded man suddenly arose and staggered across the landing, Beretta subgun in his fists. He was hit badly and knew he was dying. The guy figured the only thing left to do was try to take James with him. However, he presented an excellent target. James fired the last rounds from the Astra and drilled the Nepalese hitman in the chest. The man fell forward and tumbled down the marble stairs.

Leaning over the rail at the landing, the second mercenary pointed his M-12 blaster directly at James. Before he could trigger, his left cheekbone exploded. A 124-grain Federal Hydra-Shok projectile had crashed into his face, shattering bone. An eyesocket cracked, and the eyeball popped out to dangle from the stem of optic nerve. The mercenary did not notice. He was already dead. His corpse toppled over the rail and plunged to the ballroom floor.

DAVID MCCARTER LOWERED his Browning Hi-Power. He had emerged from his hiding place when the shooting started. He saw James was in trouble and held the Browning in a two-handed Weaver's Combat grip. An Olympic-level pistol marksman, McCarter nailed the Nepalese triggerman with a single, well-placed 9 mm round.

The pistol shot surprised a number of VIP guests. McCarter ignored their cries and the pounding of shoe leather on marble. He had discarded his tuxedo jacket and black tie to allow for greater mobility. His white silk shirt was unbuttoned at the throat. An Uzi machine pistol was hanging from a shoulder, and ammo pouches with extra magazines were clipped to his belt.

Something moved on one of the balconies. McCarter swung his Browning toward some figures in the marble box seats. Two Nepalese hitmen, armed with FAL assault rifles, were preparing to fire down at the crowd. The Phoenix placed a single pistol shot between the two gunmen. The bullet served to get their attention and discouraged them from blasting into the crowd—they would want to kill McCarter first.

McCarter switched the Hi-Power to his left hand and grabbed the Uzi with his right. He raised the machine pistol and triggered two 3-round bursts. The Briton's arm shifted from left to right, riding with the recoil instead of trying to fight it. One bullet chipped marble from a balcony rail. Five others tore into the mercenaries with fearsome force. The pair convulsed like marionettes in a madman's puppet show. Blood spilled from bullet-punctured flesh, and the gunmen collapsed among the box seats.

A scuffle occurred between two black men dressed in red jackets. McCarter rushed to the fighting waiters. The pair were struggling for the possession of a pistol. Another handgun lay on the floor near their feet. Obviously one man was a Haitian merc, and the other was one of Colonel Barama's soldiers in disguise. However, McCarter could not tell which was which.

The Phoenix pro slammed his Uzi across both men's hands to strike the pistol from their fingers. The gun clattered on the floor. The combatants stared as McCarter stepped back and pointed his Uzi at them. Both raised their hands to shoulder level.

"Who's your commanding officer?" McCarter demanded.

"Colonel Barama!" one of the men replied quickly.

"Right answer," the Briton confirmed, and suddenly kicked the other guy in the groin.

The Haitian doubled up with a breathless squeal. McCarter chopped the Uzi across the man's skull and knocked him to the floor. He turned away from the pair and allowed the soldier to gather up the pistols and cuff the dazed Haitian. There were still plenty of enemy forces to deal with. Shots were spitting from weapons in all directions as Phoenix Force and the Guyanese troops exchanged fire with the Haitian and Nepalese mercenaries who seemed to pop out of the woodwork like gun-toting roaches.

COLONEL BARAMA PUSHED back his tunic and drew a snubnose .38 S&W revolver from the holster at the small of his back. The short-barreled handgun seemed an inept toy against the enemy's automatic weapons. The colonel swung his revolver toward the dining room but held his fire when he saw Yakov Katz jog to the door.

Suddenly Barama was struck from behind. The unexpected blow knocked him to the floor. Barama turned as he fell and landed on his side, both hands wrapped around the grips of his S&W. His weapon was pointed at the person who had pushed him.

Barama was astonished to see it was George Sutcliffe. The CIA case officer looked not down at Barama but at a figure on a balcony above. A submachine gun erupted from the box seats and a network of blood-spurting holes erupted on Sutcliffe's chest. The Company man's face contorted with pain as he staggered three steps and crashed to the floor.

Rafael Encizo returned fire with his Uzi machine pistol and sprayed the balcony with a volley of 9 mm rounds. Crimson-and-gray mist spewed from the enemy gunman's bullet-shattered skull. The mercenary and his Beretta chopper fell against the rail. His lifeless form toppled over the side and dropped to the marble floor like a discarded sack of potatoes.

"Sutcliffe?" Barama hissed through clenched teeth as he crawled to the fallen CIA man.

"He's dead," Encizo declared. The Cuban had barely glanced at Sutcliffe's motionless body but had no doubt. Sutcliffe had been hit in the sternum, lungs and heart.

Encizo turned to the battle still in progress. The Cuban used a stone pillar for cover as he scanned the ballroom. The VIP guests had finally hit the floor and stayed down. The more rational members of the group had done so voluntarily, pulling their distraught companions to the floor.

A man dressed as a waiter squatted by the buffet table, a submachine gun in his fists. Encizo aimed his Uzi at the figure. Eneizo had the "waiter's" white shirt in his sights and began to squeeze the trigger. He eased up on the trigger when he noticed the target carried a Patchett subgun. The guy was one of Barama's men—at least he was armed with the same British-made weapons as the Guyanese military used.

But the Cuban realized, wasn't it possible the enemy had firearms from local black market sources as well as weapons smuggled from Brazil and Argentina?

A burst of automatic fire slashed the fellow's chest and abdomen, and he fell to the floor, convulsing in a brief tremor of death. Eneizo shifted the aim of his Uzi and spotted another figure dressed as a servant. Smoke rose from the muzzle of the man's Beretta M-12. Eneizo, not worried about shooting the wrong man this time, promptly blasted the mercenary gunman into oblivion.

"Damn it," the Cuban rasped. "Just figuring out who's on which side is difficult."

Another figure dressed as a waiter, with pistols in both hands, appeared beside the orchestra platform. Again Eneizo was unsure whether the man was friend or foe. He watched as the gunman swung his pistol toward a group of VIPs and a couple of guys dressed as waiters. Eneizo still couldn't tell whether the man was an enemy merc about to blow away the prime minster or a soldier who spotted an enemy among the guests.

Two shots bellowed behind Eneizo, and the man he had been watching was suddenly blown away. The Cuban turned and saw Barama, S&W snubnose in his fists. The colonel shuffled to the pillar and knelt beside Eneizo.

"I take it that wasn't one of your men," the Phoenix commando muttered, frustrated by the situation.

"Certainly not," Barama assured him. "I know all the soldiers I assigned here tonight. You people told me to pick only those men I knew well enough I could be reasonably sure they wouldn't be working for our enemies."

"Okay, okay," Encizo told the colonel. "Stay with me and identify your men so I don't mistake them for enemy gunmen."

"I just hope the rest of your teammates are as concerned about the safety of my men," Barama remarked.

"They'll do the best they can," Encizo assured him, "but nobody is safe in a situation like this."

GARY MANNING SPOTTED a black-clad Nepalese mercenary on a balcony, crouched among the box seats. The sharp-eyed Canadian noticed the merc carried an FAL rifle with the sling over a shoulder. The man's arms moved, but the rifle did not. Manning immediately realized the guy had to be reaching for a different kind of weapon. The Phoenix Force demolitions expert suspected what that weapon might be.

He raised and aimed his Uzi machine pistol, carefully, wishing he had a rifle. The Canadian was a superb marksman with a long gun, but was less skilled with a pistol or subgun. Nonetheless he was still far better than average with such weapons. He thumbed the selector lever of the Uzi to full-auto, hoping the greater firepower would compensate for the lack of accuracy.

Manning triggered the machine pistol. Parabellum slugs lashed the box seats in the balcony. At least two rounds struck the mercenary in the head. The goon's skull opened in a grisly spray of brains and bone fragments. His body fell from view. Relieved, Manning lowered his Uzi.

The merc's grenade exploded a split-second later.

Gary Manning had killed him, but not before the son of a bitch had pulled the pin. The explosion tore chunks of marble from the balcony and hurled them down to the ballroom below. Some of these pelted the terrified guests. Stone fragments hammered their heads and bodies. A few bloodied pieces of the slain merc also showered the crowd.

A woman screamed hysterically when she discovered a severed human hand had landed inches from her face. Muscles still twitched in the extremity, and the fingers flexed in a ghastly spasm. It resembled a large fleshy spider or a special effects gimmick from a horror film. The woman crawled from the twitching fingers and tried to run, but others held her down.

Several people suffered broken bones and scalp wounds from flying stone debris. One young diplomatic aide from Brazil climbed to his feet and ran unsteadily to a marble column, a broken forearm cradled to his chest. A killer in servant's attire spotted the man and pumped three Beretta slugs into his chest.

The assassin died a split-second after his victim hit the floor. Manning's Uzi snarled, and a trio of 9 mm rounds swept the Haitian gunman off his feet and pitched his corpse backward into the orchestra platform. The body crashed into some folding chairs, knocked over two music stands and finally came to rest on the polished wood floor.

A burst of automatic fire spat into the plaster above the Canadian's head. Manning dropped and swung his Uzi toward the threat. The gunman tried to adjust his aim, but suddenly stumbled sideways as high-velocity projectiles smashed into him. David McCarter had fired his Uzi machine pistol at the killer before Manning could respond. The Canadian warrior nodded his thanks to the Briton and dashed to the doorway of the dining room.

Katz had entered the room and was crouched by the nearest set of tables and chairs for cover. His Uzi raged at the turban-clad man in the gold jacket poised at a doorway across the room. The fellow retreated, but his fist poked around the corner with a .380 pistol to fire twice at the Israeli.

Seeing Manning at the ballroom entrance, Katz motioned to him to stay put, then gestured toward the gunman's location. Manning understood. Katz wanted to take advantage of the fact his opponent did not know the Canadian warrior had come to his assistance.

Katz took a deep breath and ran along the length of the table, away from the gunman. His arched back was barely visible above the tops of the chairs. The enemy pistolman, assuming Katz was headed for better cover and a better attacking angle, stepped from the doorway and pointed the .380 at Katz's fleeing figure.

"Hey!" Manning snapped to get the man's attention.

The guy turned and saw the muzzle-flash of Manning's Uzi—the last thing he would ever see. Parabellum slugs chopped the gunman's face to bits and splashed his fancy gold jacket with crimson blood. The phony servant dropped his pistol and reached for his ragged, brain-splattered turban. His corpse wilted to the floor before his fingers touched the headgear.

"I'll check the next room!" Katz shouted as he ran toward the fallen opponent. "You find the bomb!"

"The bomb?" Manning replied in a dazed voice.

Suddenly he knew what Katz meant. The enemy had intended to kill the prime minister and other influential guests with an explosion. It was possible they planned to enter the kitchen and ballroom with weapons blazing, but more likely a bomb would be used for the mass assassination. Perhaps a combination attack was the most likely technique: blow up the room, then gun down the survivors.

Manning glanced about the room. Several long tables with dozens of chairs stood in the center. White silk cloths draped each table. Fine china plates, soup bowls, expensive silverware and crystal was set in front of each chair. Paintings of the president and prime minister hung on the walls. Ornate chandeliers of brass and crystal dangled from the ceiling.

Was there a bomb? Where? If there was a bomb, Manning had no idea how much time was left before it would explode.

16

Heading up the stairs, Calvin James discarded the empty Astra Constable and held the Walther P-88 alertly in two hands. The battle in the ballroom was still raging, and some of the mercenary killers had struck from the balconies. This meant the enemy was upstairs as well as below. James stooped beside the slain Nepalese gunman on the landing and took the dead man's Beretta chopper.

He thrust the P-88 inside his jacket and returned it to shoulder leather. The American gripped the Italian-made M-12 submachine gun as he continued upstairs. James had used Beretta subguns before, and the weapon felt familiar in his fists. It was a compact subgun, less than seventeen inches long with the stock folded, and weighed less than eight pounds. The handgrip at the forestock, similar to the old Thompson, allowed greater control of the weapon, which had a cyclic rate of 550 r.p.m. and a blowback system similar to that of an Uzi. A 30-round magazine was fixed in the well at the front of the trigger mechanism, but James didn't know how many 9 mm cartridges were in the mag.

James reached the head of the stairs and stared into the hallway. Black and white tiles formed a checkerboard pattern on the floor. A few painted landscapes hung on the walls. Ferns rose from clay pots, and a small table against a wall contained an ashtray and some magazines. There was a row of doors along the hall, and no one else around.

"Man, I hate this," James muttered as he reached the first door and slammed a heel-kick under the knob. The lock snapped, and the door swung inward. No shots responded to the abrupt action. James swung into the room, Beretta held ready. It was a small office with two desks and a water cooler. The typewriters and telephones suggested it was a front office for secretaries. The door to the next room no doubt led to an executive office. James took a deep breath, glanced behind the two desks and marched to the next door.

"Déjà vu," James rasped, and kicked in the second door.

An angry spew of bullets tore into the door. Wood splinters hopped from the panels as James ducked by the doorway. The glare of the enemy's automatic weapon filled the dark room with bursts of light. James spotted a filing cabinet and a large globe inside the office. He had a general idea where the gunman was positioned in the room from the muzzle-flash of the subgun. James assumed the guy was probably using a desk or other large object for cover.

The commando stayed low and dove forward. He shoulder-rolled to the cabinet and globe. The enemy chopper snarled as James tumbled across the floor. Bullets chewed into the wall behind his hurtling form, but the Phoneix pro reached the cover of the cabinet unharmed. He landed on one knee by the metal file box. The globe tipped over as subgun slugs hammered it with high-velocity force.

James saw the head and shoulders of the mercenary at the corner of a desk. The muzzle-flash of his weapon illuminated the opponent's face. His dark features were fierce, eyes narrowed and teeth clenched. James snap-aimed and triggered his Beretta M-12. Three parabellum projectiles tore into the man's face. His skull burst into a ghastly plumage of brains and blood. The mercenary's corpse collapsed behind the desk.

The Phoenix commando rose from the cabinet and re-turned to the outer office. Another figure at the thresh-old was clearly visible against the light from the hall. Dressed in black cammies and a black turban, a Ne-palese mercenary stared at James and raised an Argen-tine FMK 3 submachine gun.

James nailed him with the last three rounds from the Beretta. Three scarlet holes sprouted in the Nepalese killer's chest as he fell back into the hall. The FMK slipped from his fingers as the merc sprawled across the checkerboard tiles. James headed for the fallen oppo-nent, eager to claim his FMK blaster. The weapon was an Argentine version of an Uzi, and the slain merc carried two spare ammo pouches on his belt. The Phoenix fight-er needed that extra firepower.

As James started to toss the empty M-12 aside, a great steel blade flashed from the shadows and crashed into the Beretta subgun. The unexpected blow sent the weapon flying from James's grasp. He jumped back, startled. The opponent had materialized from the darkness like a ghost. The Phoenix warrior had not heard, seen or oth-erwise sensed the attacker until the Gurkha struck. If he hadn't turned to discard the M-12 blaster, the big *kukri* knife would have decapitated him.

Captain Ajmer was impressed by James's reflexes. He did not realize the commando had blocked the knife stroke by accident rather than design. The Gurkha slashed a backhand sweep at James's chest. The agile Phoenix pro dodged the thick crescent of steel and reached for the Walther in shoulder leather. Ajmer raised his *kukri*.

James stepped back, aware if he drew his pistol the mercenary could chop his hand off with the long, heavy curved blade. At close quarters the big knife was as effective as a gun. The American needed to put some distance between himself and the Gurkha before he could bring the Walther into play. However, Ajmer surprised him again by kicking him in the abdomen.

The commando doubled over, realizing he had concentrated on the knife more than the position of his opponent. James was rattled by the suddenness of the attacker and his phantomlike stealth.

Captain Ajmer was real enough, and so was his *kukri*. The Gurkha swung the blade at James's head, determined to chop it open like an oversized grapefruit. The black commando grabbed his opponent's wrists to hold the knife at bay. They struggled, the blade held high. Ajmer tried to force his wrists against James's thumbs to break the grasp, but the black warrior held on and stamped a heel into his enemy's shin.

James whipped a knee to the Gurkha's belly and turned sharply to try to wrench the knife from the mercenary's grasp. Ajmer, pivoting, suddenly bent his knees and dropped. As his rump hit the floor, he thrust a boot to James's knee. The tactic was a variation of a judo sit-down throw. James hadn't encountered this technique in years, and the throw caught him off balance. He toppled sideways to the floor as the captain yanked free of his grasp.

The Phoenix warrior landed on his shoulder and hip. He glimpsed the steel arch descending and pulled his head aside. The heavy blade chopped into the floor near his right ear. James smashed his fist to the bridge of Ajmer's nose. The merc groaned and staggered back. The *kukri* popped free from the floor. James sprang to his feet next to a desk as Ajmer, hissing with rage, launched another attack.

James swiftly scooped up the manual typewriter from the desk and heaved it into his opponent. The heavy machine crashed into Ajmer's chest and sent him stumbling backward. James charged and swung a roundhouse kick to the mercenary's wrist. The *kukri* dropped from numbed fingers as James slashed a cross-body karate chop to the Gurkha's upper lip. Blood filled the merc's mouth, and he staggered into a wall. James kept on the offensive and planted a hard side-kick to Ajmer's stomach.

The Gurkha's hands clamped around James's ankle, twisting hard. The commando hopped on one foot and tried to maintain his balance. Tricky little bastard, James thought, and pushed off the floor with his single leg. The Phoenix pro whirled in midair and turned in the direction of the ankle twist, the heel of his free leg slamming into the side of Ajmer's skull. Both men went down. James broke his fall with his hands and rolled away. Ajmer dropped to his knees, stunned and bewildered, unsure what had happened to fill his head with throbbing pain.

Ajmer spotted his *kukri* and crawled to it. As soon as his fingers closed around the buffalo handle, he climbed to his feet, the big knife once more in his fist. James knelt by a desk, one hand inside his jacket. He pulled out the Walther P-88 and pointed it at Ajmer.

The Gurkha glanced at the gun and smiled slightly. Then he attacked, knife held high. James squeezed the trigger and shot Ajmer dead-center in the heart. The merc kept coming. James shot him again. Ajmer twitched but continued his lunge toward the Phoenix crusader.

James dove to the floor and rolled away as the Gurkha swung. His heavy blade chopped into the edge of the desk. Ajmer slumped to the floor. His fingers released the knife, which remained lodged in the desk. Staring down at the Gurkha, James almost pumped him with another parabellum to be certain he was dead.

"Okay," James said breathlessly as he backed away from the corpse. "I figure you won't be gettin' up again, after all."

GARY MANNING PEERED under the long center table in the dining room. He had assumed the longest table would be the one selected for the most honored guests. Manning checked beneath the head of the table for a bomb, but found nothing.

As the Canadian demolitions expert prepared to check the other tables, he considered what was known about their opponents. Wilkens was a Nazi who quoted *Mein Kampf* as if it was scripture. Such a man would also be a student of the life of Adolf Hitler. Manning recalled there had been an unsuccessful attempt to assassinate Hitler by members of his own military command. A bomb in an attaché case had been placed under a table in a meeting room. The explosion had injured everyone except Hitler, because the German *Fuhrer* had unexpectedly left the meeting a moment before the blast.

To Wilkens, bombs under tables were probably unreliable. Of course, the Nepalese or Haitian mercs had probably planted the bomb, but Wilkens would have instructed them. Manning gazed up at the chandeliers. An explosion among the light fixtures would certainly blast shards of shattered crystal throughout the room. The shrapnel damage would be terrible, but unlikely to cause large numbers of deaths. To ensure high casualties, the chandeliers would have to be rigged with large amounts of explosives. These would be too obvious for any experienced demolitions man to use.

Manning considered other possibilities. He even began to wonder whether there was an explosive concealed in the dining hall. The sound of automatic fire told him the battle was still in progress within the building. Manning didn't want to waste time looking for a hypothetical bomb when his fellow Phoenix warriors were still at risk.

But then he remembered Katz's assured tone. "You find the bomb!" the Israeli commando had called. If there was a bomb, Manning didn't know how much time he had left to find it. The bomb might have a timing mechanism, but the Canadian guessed it would probably have a radio detonator so that it could be set off only when the potential targets were assembled in the room. That would explain why the bomb had not already exploded. But would the enemy still detonate the damn thing?

Manning's gaze fell upon the portaits of the president and prime minister, which overlooked the tables. An explosion from the direction of the portraits would certainly destroy anyone seated at the head of the long table and probably many others. Manning hurried to the president's portrait, gripped the gold frame and pushed up to lift it from the wall.

Lowering it to the floor, he turned it over. The wooden back was covered by a thick layer of a white doughlike substance. A small black box was lodged in the plastic explosives, with a wire antenna taped to the frame. Manning recognized the object as a miniature radio detonator with a special blasting cup attached. It was a simple matter to remove the detonator and blasting cap. Manning tossed them aside and took the second portrait from the wall. He found more plastic explosives and another radio detonator.

The Canadian deactivated the bomb and discarded the receiver unit and blaster. Relieved, he propped the painting against the wall. Suddenly he was startled by two loud bangs, like pistol shots. White light burst from the floor as bits of plastic and metal pelted the Phoenix commando's legs. The blasting caps had exploded a split-second apart. Someone had set off the radio detonators.

"If I had the time, I swear I'd have a nervous breakdown," Manning muttered, his heart pounding wildly.

GUILLOTIN CURSED as he pressed the button to a radio transmitter unit. The Haitian threw it to the floor with disgust. He glared at Chirac, the so-called explosives expert. Guillotin shook his head and reached for his Beretta M-12 on the counter by the sink.

"I didn't hear any explosions," he growled. "Did you?"

"Something must have gone wrong," Chirac replied with a nervous shrug. The demolitions man feared Guillotin's murderous temper. "I'm certain I prepared the explosives correctly. The radio detonators should have set off the RDX compound."

"Obviously it did not work," Guillotin hissed. "I should have known anything moderately complex would be too much for you to handle."

Chirac was sure whatever had gone wrong with the explosives was not his fault, but he didn't argue with the Ton Ton Macoute leader. Guillotin was shrewd and intelligent, yet also incredibly ruthless and brutal. Chirac had seen ample proof of that since they had entered the kitchen at Wellington Hall.

The Haitians had surprised the two soldiers stationed at the kitchen entrance, as well as the cooks and dishwashers. Guillotin, Chirac and the Nepalese merc in the gold jacket had rounded up the group at gunpoint and marched them into the refrigerated locker. There was no need for Guillotin to draw his machete from its sheath and chop off the heads of the soldiers, but he did it anyway. Maybe just to convince the kitchen personnel to keep their mouths shut and obey orders. Maybe he did it because decapitation was his trademark.

Guillotin locked the cooks and dishwasher in the freezer with the headless corpses of the murdered soldiers. Chirac shivered as he watched Guillotin calmly pick up the severed heads by the hair and deposit them in the sink as if handling cabbages. The Ton Ton boss then cleaned the blood from his machete and returned it to the sheath. Chopping off the soldiers' heads didn't seem to bother him any more than slicing into a loaf of bread.

However, Guillotin no longer appeared calm. The exchange of gunfire throughout the building signaled that their plans had gone sour. The explosives had also failed to detonate. Both men felt trapped, like cornered animals about to be netted and speared.

Suddenly a figure appeared at the doors. A middle-aged white man, dressed in a tuxedo and gray gloves, kicked open one of the doors. He held an Uzi machine pistol in his left fist, braced across his right arm. Guillotin immediately jumped behind a table for cover. Chirac dropped to one knee and swung his subgun at the opponent. Yakov Katz triggered his Uzi before the Haitian could get off a shot.

A burst of 9 mm slugs cut open Chirac from solar plexus to throat. The impact drove him back into the table. Pots and pans rattled from the utility rack, and Chirac's submachine gun clattered on the floor. Guillotin saw the demolitions man slide lifelessly to the tiles. He thrust his M-12 around the table and fired.

Katz retreated as bullets raked the doors and framework. He kicked open the other door to divert his opponent, then poked his Uzi through the opening and triggered another burst. Only two shots spat from the muzzle—the last two rounds from the magazine.

Guillotin realized the white man's Uzi was empty. He also guessed the white man would either attempt to reload or draw a backup piece. The Haitian figured his best option was to rush his opponent before he could fire back at him. Guillotin jumped from cover and, training his Beretta on the doors, charged the commando's position.

The Israeli thrust his arm through the doorway and pointed a gloved index finger at the Haitian. Guillotin almost laughed at this absurd gesture. What did this white idiot think he was doing? Casting a curse on Guillotin like the ignorant peasants in Haiti who prayed to their voodoo deities or the Christian God for protection? Neither religion had ever helped save anyone from Guillotin before, and he was confident no spirits would rescue Katz now.

The shot astonished Guillotin. A small-caliber projectile punched through his chest and punctured a lung. The unexpected pain was so great he staggered across the room and dropped his Beretta subgun. He placed both hands to his chest, half-expecting to find the wound was not real. Katz entered the kitchen, right arm extended. Smoke curled from the torn cloth at the end of his index finger.

"Merde!" Guillotin exclaimed in stunned disbelief. How could a man shoot him with a finger?

The Haitian didn't realize Katz's right arm was a prosthesis with a .22 Magnum one-shot pistol built into it with the "index finger" as the barrel. Katz kept the "finger" pointed at Guillotin's face as he reached inside his tuxedo jacket with his left hand.

Suddenly Guillotin realized what had happened. He also guessed Katz was only reaching for a pistol because the finger gun was out of ammo. Bellowing with rage, the Haitian launched himself at the Israeli. Anger and determination overpowered the burning pain in his chest as Guillotin yanked the machete from his belt. The long heavy blade slashed at Katz's extended right arm.

The Israeli swung his prosthesis out of the path of the sharp steel and stepped back, drawing his Walter P-88. Guillotin abruptly snapped his wrist and slapped the flat of the machete blade across the barrel of Katz's pistol. The blow struck the Walther from his hand. Guillotin raised his machete and prepared to swing the sharp blade at the Phoenix commander's head.

Katz suddenly stepped forward and lashed his prosthesis in a cross-body stroke. The side of his steel hand hit Guillotin just under the bullet hole in his chest. The blow sent a terrible wave of agony through the Haitian's body and ruptured bullet-torn tissue in a lung. Blood rose up his throat and into his mouth. The Israeli grabbed his opponent's wrist to hold back the machete as he drove a knee between the Haitian's legs.

Guillotin convulsed in pain and vomited crimson on his shirtfront. His knees buckled as his crotch seemed to explode. Katz slapped his steel palm against the mercenary's skull and slashed across Guillotin's wrist. Bones popped, and the machete dropped from the Haitian's fingers. Katz bent his right elbow and rammed it into the Haitian's solar plexus. Guillotin started to double up from the blow, but Katz whipped a vicious backhanded blow to his opponent's face.

The steel extremity struck with the force of a rifle butt and sent Guillotin hurtling across to the sink counter. Blood oozed from his mouth and nostrils, his chest felt about to cave in, his legs seemed made of rubber. The Haitian gripped the rim of the sink to brace himself and remain on his feet. His vision was blurred, but he recognized the round, hair-covered dome of a severed head in the sink.

A large meat cleaver lay on a cutting board on the counter. Guillotin coughed up a glob of blood and snot. The Ton Ton killer knew he could not last much longer. He had one last chance to take out the older, one-armed opponent. Guillotin grabbed the head by the hair with one hand and reached for the cleaver with the other. He whirled and threw the severed head at Katz.

The Phoenix commando dodged the grisly projectile, too experienced in dealing with the unexpected to allow the ghastly missile to slow down his reflexes. Guillotin stumbled forward, the meat cleaver in his fist. Quickly Katz stooped, grabbed the discarded machete, rose and swung the big jungle knife.

A rising diagonal cut caught Guillotin at the wrist. It chopped through muscle and bone to take the hand off at the joint. The Haitian screamed as he saw his own fist sail through the air, fingers still clutching the handle of the cleaver. Blood fountained from the stump of his wrist. Guillotin threw back his head and bellowed.

Again Katz swung his prosthesis and slammed it across Guillotin's exposed throat. The blow crushed his windpipe and sent the Haitian back into the sink. The Ton

Ton Macoute boss slumped into a seated position on the floor. His eyes swelled in their sockets, and he twitched slightly as his life seeped away. He was vaguely aware that he had inflicted monstrous agony on countless others in the past and there was brutal justice in his slow and painful death. Guillotin clung to his last bitter and ironic thought as his mind plunged into the final blackness of oblivion.

"Bloody hell!" McCarter exclaimed as he stepped into the kitchen.

The Briton was accustomed to scenes of violence, but he wasn't prepared for the carnage in the kitchen. Bloodied corpses littered the crimson-stained tiles, walls and cabinets. A severed head lay on one side, features mashed and distorted. Guillotin's amputated hand had opened like a five-petal flower from hell, the meat cleaver positioned on the palm. McCarter shook his head and looked at Katz.

"Whatever they planned to have for dinner, I think I'll pass," he remarked.

"I don't hear any shooting," the Israeli declared. "Is the battle over?"

"Oh, yeah," McCarter confirmed. "And the other side definitely lost. Barama lost some men, and a few of the guests are injured. At least two are dead. The mercenaries are pretty well wiped out, and Goddard has been placed under arrest. The bad news is Wilkens got away. His limo left before the shooting started."

"He won't get far," Katz stated. "Let's talk to Barama and the prime minister about getting an assault force together to go after that Nazi bastard."

"Reckon he'll head back to his plantation?" McCarter inquired.

"I don't think he's got anywhere else to go," the Phoenix leader replied.

They heard fists pounding on metal and voices calling for help. The commandos turned toward the freezer. McCarter walked to the door and yanked back the latch. His Uzi ready, he turned the handle and pulled the door open. The cooks and dishwashers emerged from the frigid tomb, trembling teeth chattering out of control.

"Oh, God," one of the cooks said, gasping for air and staring at Katz and McCarter as if they were angels sent to deliver him from damnation. "There's no way we can thank you!"

"Don't worry about that," McCarter said cheerfully. "You blokes just clean up the kitchen, and we'll call it even."

The Phoenix warriors left the room. A startled scream revealed that one of the kitchen crew had discovered just how bad a mess they had left behind.

17

Otto Weissflog marched into his plantation house, his tuxedo jacket slung over a shoulder, his bow tie undone. The Nazi madman tossed the jacket onto the newel post at the bottom of the stairs. Werner and Reinhard followed their boss into the hall, their tux jackets and ties already discarded. Both carried Beretta submachine guns. Karin Weissflog, pale and frightened, entered the house and stood at the doorway.

"Reinhard," Weissflog began as he turned to his men. "Assemble the troops. Have them in formation outside the billets. I'll address them on the P.A. system. Tell them to get ready to defend the plantation."

"We could head for the Pakaraima Mountains," Reinhard suggested. "From there we could cross the border to Brazil. Our comrades there can give us shelter at their strongholds in the Amazon..."

"None of them would help us now," Weissflog told him. "The Nazi cells are fragmented and worried about their survival. If we had succeeded in overthrowing the government of Guyana, our comrades would swarm to us. Now we'll be treated as lepers."

"Still," Reinhard insisted, "we would have a better chance in Brazil than here."

"The Guyana Defense Forces will guard the borders and will no doubt contact the Brazilian government and urge them to do likewise," Weissflog stated.

"Perhaps we're assuming too much, *Mein Herr*," Werner suggested, trying to sound hopeful. "True, we heard shooting at Wellington Hall when we drove from Georgetown, but we don't know Guillotin and Ajmer lost the battle. Perhaps they won."

"They would have contacted us by radio," Weissflog said, and shook his head. "*Nein*, Werner. We must assume the mercenaries failed and prepare for our final battle."

"*Ich verstehe*," Werner said grimly. "I understand."

"*Sehr gut*," the Nazi leader replied. "Very good. Now, contact the sentries by radio and tell them to stay alert and watch for any sign of danger. Tell them reinforcements will help them defend the plantation. No need to say more than that. After you finish, I want you to get the women and children into the bomb shelter."

"*Ja, Mein Herr*," Werner said with a nod.

"The shelter isn't large enough for all the men," Weissflog stated. "However, you both may go to the shelter. You have served me with loyalty and courage for many years. If you choose to save yourselves, I will understand."

"We will remain with you to the end," Werner declared.

Reinhard nodded in agreement.

"I appreciate your loyalty," Weissflog told them. "Let us all die as we have lived. The soldiers of the Aryan race should die fighting."

"What do you think you're fighting for?" Karin demanded, unable to stay quiet any longer.

She approached her husband, eyes fixed on Weissflog with accusation and sorrow. Werner and Reinhard decided it was best to leave the couple to talk privately for what little time remained. The bodyguards departed to tend to their duties. Weissflog saw the pain and anger in his wife's face.

"I thought you understood, Karin," he said. "We spent our lives fighting a just and righteous cause. Just as our fathers did. Your father as well as mine."

"Our fathers?" Karin glared at her spouse. "That's what this has all been about from the beginning. We've been carrying out our fathers' wishes all our lives. They taught us their version of the truth. They taught us we were superior to others because of our background and racial heritage."

"There is nothing wrong with *volkisch* pride," Weissflog declared.

Karin rolled her eyes toward the ceiling. *Volkisch* had been another pet word of Otto's father. It meant "folkish," but to the Nazis it took on properties of nationalism and racism. Her husband had been brainwashed by a propaganda campaign that began the day he was born.

"This has always been more than pride," Karin insisted. "Our fathers raised us with their obsessions about world domination, Aryan supremacy and total arrogance that Hitler was right and the rest of the world was wrong."

"You're upset and I understand that," Weissflog said sadly. "I feel I have failed you and young Gerhart. For that, I am very sorry. I failed my father and the dreams he passed on to me."

"Dreams you never truly shared, Otto," Karin said. Her eyes brimmed with tears that overflowed and began to stream down her cheeks. "Why couldn't you have pursued your own dreams instead? I saw how you suffered trying to follow these goals of conquest. All the killing and scheming ate at your soul like a cancer.''

''My father's *Willensmeinung* reached out from the grave,'' Weissflog answered. ''Just as *der Fuhrer* commanded an entire generation of Germans, so I was commanded to follow my father. His dreams were too great to allow any room for my own.''

Karin closed her eyes and shook her head. Even now, Weissflog was clinging to the doctrine of Hitler and *Mein Kampf* although he realized this philosophy had destroyed him. The term *Willensmeinung* was believed to have been invented by Adolf Hitler. Roughly translated, it means ''an opinion of will.'' Karin wished Otto Weissflog had been concerned with his own opinion and had believed in his own will instead of simply obeying that of his father and the fanatical creed expressed in *Mein Kampf*.

''It didn't have to be this way,'' Karin said as she covered her face with her hands and wept. ''Why wasn't it different?''

Weissflog placed a hand on his wife's shoulder and embraced her. Then he pushed her away.

''I want you to go to the shelter now,'' he urged. ''I'll send Gerhart there, too. Try to teach our son not to follow his father's footsteps. That hasn't worked out too well for the Weissflog family.''

He slipped a hand under her chin and stared at her tear-filled blue eyes.

''I have to accept what my actions have brought upon me,'' Weissflog declared. ''My regrets won't change anything. I can't blame my father or anyone else for what I've done. The one thing I don't regret is that I married you.''

He held her close. Karin sobbed against his chest. Weissflog kissed her forehead and stepped away from his wife. She wanted to say something, but knew nothing could help. Her husband headed for his den.

She recalled the stories of Norse mythology, a favorite form of entertainment of her father. The Nazi could relate to the legends of the Viking gods. Teutonic supermen filled the myths of the Norsemen. Karin remembered the most disturbing of the legends.

Ragnarök—the final battle between the gods and the giants. Both sides were destroyed in the conflict. Karin trembled, aware that the plantation would soon be the setting for the Weissflog's own *Ragnarök*.

THE SENTRIES WERE WARNED that the plantation could be attacked by a large, well-armed force before dawn. A pair of guards stationed by a barbed wire fence along the fields of sugarcane received the message from their field radio. Werner had delivered the message. It would have been serious enough if the officer on guard duty issued the alert. The fact one of Weissflog's personal aides had contacted them suggested the order had come directly from Weissflog himself.

Both men were armed with FAL automatic rifles. They made certain their weapons were loaded with full magazines, rounds chambered and selectors set on full-auto. Rifles ready, they scanned the road and surrounding jungle. Even the acres of tall sugarcane suddenly seemed sinister. The familiar stalks resembled enemy lances. Although they were accustomed to the smell of the moist earth and rotting vegetation used as fertilizer, the scent now reminded them of death and decay.

Werner had said reinforcements would be sent to the guard posts. The sentries knew this meant Weissflog expected some serious and extremely formidable opposition. They would be relieved when more soldiers arrived to back them up. Trained as storm troopers, the sentries had spent most of their lives preparing for combat, but the thought of confronting an organized, well-armed assault force frightened them more than either man would admit. War games and swooping down on unarmed villages was hardly the same as facing other soldiers on a battlefield.

"What is that?" one of the guards asked with a gasp.

The other man followed the pointing finger of his comrade and saw the oval-shaped white lights on the road. They appeared to be headlights, yet seemed to be spaced too far apart to belong to a car or truck. A rumble of engines and metal treads against earth alarmed the pair. They saw the huge dark shape of the vehicle as it drew closer. The rig resembled a rolling pillbox with a cannon extended from the top.

"*Gott!*" the sentry exclaimed. "It is a tank!"

The sentries stared in horror as another tank appeared behind the first. A deuce-and-a-half army truck followed the big armor-plated monsters. The FAL rifles seemed powerless against such awesome might. One storm trooper watched the vehicles through a pair of field glasses while the other headed for the guard shack to report the discovery to headquarters.

"Freeze and drop your weapons!" a voice ordered. The command was repeated in German to be sure the sentries understood.

The guard near the shack began to move behind the shed for cover and swung his rifle toward the sound of the voice. The man heard something rip the air with a sharp serpentine hiss and felt a terrible pain in the center of his chest. He glanced down at the short fiberglass shaft that extended from under his breastbone. Cyanide seeped from the tip of the shaft into the man's blood. The sentry's pain ended almost as soon as it began. His heart tightened in a cyanide death lock, and he collapsed, unfired FAL still in his fists.

"Drop it or you'll join him!" the voice warned.

The other sentry dropped his rifle and raised his hands.

Gary Manning stepped from behind the trunk of a greenheart tree. The Canadian commando, wearing black cammies, paratrooper boots and a black knit cap, pointed an FAL rifle at the sentry. A foot-long silencer was attached to the barrel, a Starlite scope mounted to the frame. David McCarter appeared behind the Canadian, clad in the same attire, Barnett Commando crossbow in his fists. Manning covered the sentry while the Briton walked to the fence and snipped through the barbed wire with a pair of cutters.

"Hit the dirt," Manning told the guard. "Face down on your belly. *Schnell!*"

The sentry obeyed, and McCarter bound his wrists together behind his back, then frisked him to be certain he was unarmed. Manning headed for the road that stretched across the vast wet acres of sugarcane. The Canadian demolitions expert set a small charge by the gate. The tanks could easily crash through the barrier, but the gate could be booby-trapped. Manning intended to clear the entrance before the armored vehicles reached the gate.

Manning jogged back to the guard shack and waited. Three seconds later, the timer triggered the detonator and blasting cap to ignite the C-4 plastic explosives. The blast tore the gate apart. There was no booby trap, but now Manning could be certain the lead tank would not be damaged and the men inside injured or killed. McCarter gathered up the sentries' weapons and made certain the surviving guard was securely bound.

The tanks rolled through the gate. The Guyanese government and the Guyana Defense Forces had responded to the assassination attempts at Wellington Hall swiftly and without reservation. The prime minister, the president and other leaders of the national government had authorized the military to use whatever force was necessary to take Wilkens's plantation fortress. The military was not taking chances. The tanks were proof of this.

Guyana had purchased half a dozen Bernardini MB-3 TAMOYO tanks from Brazil in 1985. All six were involved in the raid on the plantation. The Brazilian-made tanks were not the most advanced armored vehicles in the world, but they were very impressive. Painted in a brown and green camouflage pattern, each TAMOYO was equipped with machine guns and a 105 mm cannon with 18 rounds ready-to-fire in the turret and an additional 50 rounds reserved in the hull.

Two TAMOYO tanks and a truck full of troops hit the plantation from the sugarcane fields. Another pair of armored MB-3 rigs and more Guyanese soldiers were ready to attack from the main road. The remaining pair of tanks were posted two kilometers away, along with more than a hundred soldiers. The Guyana Defense Forces consisted of approximately seventeen hundred members. More than two hundred had been mobilized that night for the raid.

Phoenix Force had divided into two groups to assist the Guyanese troops. Manning and McCarter joined the unit commanded by Colonel Barama. The other three Phoenix commandos were with the second assault unit. Hitting a base with tanks was not typical for Phoenix Force, but they had persuaded the military to allow them to participate. The Guyanese forces were green troops commanded by officers who simply wanted a victory. They would be tempted to blast everyone and everything at the plantation.

However, Phoenix Force had two major concerns about an all-out attack on the plantation. Wilkens employed a large number of laborers. At least thirty lived in a set of cottage-style houses at the plantation. These laborers weren't Nazis and didn't deserve to be blown to bits because of their employer. The wives and children of the Nazis were also noncombatants, and Phoenix Force wanted to spare them if possible. Finally, Wilkens— whom Goddard told them was actually Otto Weissflog—had assembled young Nazi followers from other strongholds in Brazil, Argentina, Bolivia and Paraguay. Weissflog might have records and maps that could help locate these Nazi bases in the future. The five-man commando team didn't want Weissflog's house destroyed until they could locate such vital information.

Manning and McCarter watched the tanks roll by. The truck stopped, and both men climbed into the cab. The driver grimly pursued the tanks as Manning pulled up the antenna to a walkie-talkie radio unit.

"Hannibal One, this is Hannibal Two," the Canadian spoke into the radio. "Do you read me? Over."

"This is Hannibal One," Katz's voice replied. "Read you loud and clear. Over."

"We're inside," Manning stated. "The enemy probably knows we're here. I blasted the gate and I assume someone noticed. Even if they didn't, they'll all know we're here very soon. Over."

"They'll know it from this direction, too," Katz assured him. "We're ready to move. Over."

"Just ask the guys on the guns to be careful where they throw those tank shells," Manning urged. "I'd hate to get killed by friendly fire. Over and out."

The caravan continued through the plantation. Two sets of headlights appeared on the road ahead. British Land Rovers, loaded with storm troopers, had been sent to assist the sentries. They did not expect to encounter armored tanks on the road. A Nazi opened fire with a machine gun mounted to the roll bar of a Rover. Bullets pelted the lead tank without causing as much as a dent in the armor.

The cannon roared in response. Flame ejected from the muzzle of the tank's gun. The shell hit one of the Land Rovers directly in the hood. The big high-explosive round exploded on impact, and the Rover burst apart as if it was made of fragile glass. Chunks of metal and flaming gasoline flew in all directions. Debris fell in the cane fields. The other Rover, bowled over by the explosion, rolled off the road into the sugarcane.

A soldier opened the hatch to the turret and grabbed the trigger grips of the machine gun mounted above the gun base. He trained the weapon on the fallen vehicle and opened fire. One of the storm troopers screamed as bullets ripped into his flesh. Another was pinned under the Rover, and a third lay sprawled near the wreck, his neck broken.

Another salvo of machine gun rounds burst the gas tank and sparked metal. Flames ignited and the fuel tank exploded. Fire crackled among the stalks of sugarcane. The flames were all that stirred among the crops as the TAMOYO behemoths and the transport truck rolled on.

THE CARAVAN APPROACHED a row of shanties and a smaller crop of citrus fruit trees. Another Land Rover was parked by the small dwellings. Two uniformed white men stood near the vehicle, holding assault rifles. A group of black men, women and a few children squatted between the shacks in search of shelter. The storm troopers pointed their weapons at the tanks. The lead TAMOYO slowly swung its cannon at the enemy.

"Throw down your weapons and surrender!" Colonel Barama's voice boomed from an amplifier. "You can't win! How do you think you can fight these tanks?"

The two storm troopers responded by firing at the tanks. Bullets raked the armored vehicles as the pair charged forward. One man continued to fire his rifle at the TAMOYO giants as his comrade heaved a hand grenade at the first tank. It exploded near the mighty vehicle with little effect except to unnerve the men inside—including Barama.

"Don't return fire!" Manning shouted into his walkie-talkie as he opened the door to the truck cab and hurried outside. "Don't do it, Barama! A shell could kill the other people by the houses! Hold your fire!"

The Canadian dropped to one knee and braced the stock of his FAL to his shoulder. Quickly he fixed the Starlite scope on the advancing storm troopers. The cross hairs found an opponent's head. Manning squeezed the trigger. He felt the familiar recoil of the rifle and saw his target's head snap to one side.

After his comrade fell, the other storm trooper swung his weapon toward the truck. He was still looking for the marksman who took out his partner when Manning pumped another FAL round through his heart. The Canadian watched the second man fall, confident he would not rise again. The hatch of the lead tank rose, and Colonel Barama emerged.

"You handled that well," he admitted. "What do we do with those people?"

The colonel pointed at the frightened laborers clustered by the shanties. They appeared to be unsure whether to hide or flee for their lives. Manning doubted they presented any danger. They certainly didn't look like Haitian mercenaries, and the black hired help would hardly fit in as members of Weissflog's Nazi force.

"Order some of your men to round them up for questioning and keep an eye on them until the battle is over," Manning suggested. "If more of Weissflog's stooges show up, these folks might need protection."

"I hate to use my men as baby-sitters," Barama remarked.

"Hell, Colonel," McCarter spoke up. "We brought tanks and backup troops. The reinforcements include howitzers and three gunships. I think you can spare a few men."

"Don't underestimate the enemy, Mr. Carver," Barama declared. "I would have thought you'd know that by now."

"I don't underestimate anyone," the Briton assured him. "But we already know we've got the Nazi outmanned and outgunned this time."

"You sound almost disappointed," Manning remarked as he climbed back into the truck. "Does it bother you that we're finally taking on opponents with all the odds in our favor instead of the other way around?"

"Reckon it doesn't feel quite like a fair fight," McCarter admitted, and joined his partner in the cab.

"Yeah," Manning agreed, "but I think I could get used to it."

Barama ordered several soldiers to stay with the laborers. The rest of the attack force continued to travel the dirt road through the plantation. They drew steadily closer to the center of the property, where Otto Weiss-flog and his Nazi Stormtroopers would make their final stand.

18

Hannibal One reached the destination before Barama's unit. Around the mansion and surrounding billets at the core of the Wilkens plantation, the Nazis had set up machine gun nests surrounded with walls of sandbags. Riflemen were posted on rooftops and at windows and doors of the barracks.

Weissflog's storm troopers had received many hours of training. They had been taught survival in the jungles, search-and-destroy operations in urban areas and techniques for combating the resistance Weissflog had anticipated after the Nazis took power. However, his forces had not seized power in Georgetown. The storm troopers' training had concentrated on how to hold military control after conquering a small nation. Little attention had been paid to defense of the plantation itself.

And no one had expected the place to be attacked by tanks.

Rifles and machine guns fired at the TAMOYO juggernauts with less effect than a pellet pistol would have on a bull elephant. The big 105 mm guns bellowed, and tank shells crashed into the billets. Rooftops blasted loose, and wooden walls collapsed. Mangled and dismembered Nazi corpses were splattered across the compound.

One ambitious young storm trooper approached a tank from the rear, climbing onto the shell and moving to the turret. The Nazi took a grenade from his belt as he tried to reach the hatch. If he could get it open, the enemy soldier planned to drop the blaster inside, where the TAMOYO's thick armor could not protect its occupants. Indeed the confines presented no opportunity of escape or cover. The crew would be chopped into human hamburger—extremely rare.

He didn't notice the figure in black camouflage on foot. The man braced an Uzi machine pistol across his prosthesis, aimed at the storm trooper and opened fire. Parabellum rounds slammed into the young fanatic and sent his body tumbling across the body of the tank. He pulled the pin from the grenade as he fell. It exploded by the tank's row of wheels and tractor treads.

Yako Katz did not check to see whether the tank had been damaged. The crew was still alive because he'd taken care of the storm trooper. If they had to contend with a "flat tire," that was a small price for their lives. Calvin James followed the Phoenix commander on foot. They saw the other two tanks and personnel truck of Hannibal Two approach from the sugarcane fields.

"Man, these dudes are gettin' clobbered," James remarked as he watched the barracks burn.

The 105 mm tank shells hadn't left much of the billets. Flames danced among the charred remains of the ruined structures. Chunks of pipe poked among wooden kindling here and there. Pieces of human debris also littered the site. A handful of storm troopers who had survived now launched a desperate charge in hope of reaching the armored rigs and somehow stopping the great war machines.

Rafael Encizo spotted two attackers and sprayed them with a burst of Uzi slugs. The pair twisted about in a horrid jitterbug of death. Encizo dove behind a tank for cover as the barrel of a light machine gun appeared above a column of sandbags.

A barrage of high-velocity rounds hammered the TAMOYO. Bullets whined against steel, and Encizo heard the ricochets rocket past. The Cuban was not in a good position to retaliate. However, Calvin James had the machine gun nest in his sights as he leaned around the rear of the other tank.

The black commando carried an M-16 assault rifle with an M-203 grenade launcher attached to the under-side of the barrel. He judged the distance to the sand-bag, aimed with care and triggered the M-203. A 40 mm cartridge-style grenade sailed across the compound and descended on the machine gun nest like a killer comet.

The grenade shell exploded. Sandbags hurled from the mound. The machine gun soared twenty feet before it crashed to earth. The ragged corpse of a storm trooper was also pitched from the nest. The body, which traveled almost as far as the battered machine gun, hit the ground as lifeless as a sack of sawdust.

A tank shell burst through the side of the mansion. Walls caved in, and flames danced inside the house. A submachine gun protruded from an upstairs window. Katz fired up at the Beretta chopper, and it spun from its holder's fingers. Blood-streaked arms dangled from the window.

The lead tank of Hannibal Two rolled forward and pointed its cannon at the mansion. Katz grabbed the walkie-talkie from his belt and switched on the radio. Manning's voice was already on the wavelength.

"Don't use the tank gun, Colonel," the Canadian urged.

"That's right," Katz added. "There may be women and innocent children in there as well as Nazi records. Hold your fire."

"All right," Barama's voice replied. "I'll try to talk them out. If that doesn't work, we'll use the machine gun instead of the cannon."

Gary Manning and David McCarter emerged from the truck and as they headed for the lead tank, spotted Katz by one of the Hannibal One tanks. James appeared behind the same vehicle. The Canadian and Briton jogged to their partners. The rumble of tank engines nearly drowned out their voices. The TAMOYOs were rolling into position to cover the house on all sides. Guyanese troops dashed through the compound with weapons held ready as they checked for survivors among the enemy.

"Where's Rafael?" McCarter inquired as he checked the magazine to his Uzi machine pistol. The Briton had left his crossbow at the truck.

"He's okay," James assured him. "The Nazis are just about wiped out. Guess they weren't prepared for anything like this."

"Weissflog gambled on his scheme to assassinate the people at Wellington Hall and he lost," Katz stated. "It appears he lost everything."

"We won't know until we get in that house," Manning said.

The amplified voice of Colonel Barama boomed from the TAMOYO tank. "Stanley Wilkens!" he began. "You can't escape! You're beaten! Surrender or we'll blow your house apart!"

No answer came from the mansion.

"They blew a hole in the wall," Manning commented as he lowered his FAL rifle and grabbed the Uzi that hung from a shoulder strap. "I'm going in."

"I'm with you, mate," McCarter declared with a nod.

"Give Cal and I enough time to get around back," Katz urged. "We'll find a way in from that direction. High probability Weissflog wouldn't have his wife on the top floors of the house. Probably sent her and maybe other women and children to the basement or some other place of relative safety."

"Yeah," Manning agreed. He keyed his walkie-talkie. "Barama? You read me?"

"Yes," the colonel's voice replied. "We're about to open fire on the house, unless you have some objections."

"Just shoot high," Manning replied. "We're going in low. Don't want to catch any stray rounds. Okay?"

"Understood," Barama assured him. "Be careful, gentlemen."

"Careful?" James snorted. "How can we do this crazy shit and still be careful when we do it?"

"Try not to get killed," Manning answered.

THE TAMOYO'S MACHINE GUN snarled and blasted a stream of rapid-fire rounds at the mansion's second-story windows. Katz and James bolted from cover and ran around the building. Manning pulled the pin from a concussion grenade and lobbed it at the front door. The blast kicked in the door and smashed windows. A storm trooper staggered through the archway onto the porch, assault rifle in one hand, his other hand clasped to the bleeding gash on his face.

Dashing toward the house, McCarter fired his Uzi into his dazed opponent. The storm trooper's arms flung wide, and his head snapped back, mouth open in a silent scream. The man fell and rolled down the steps.

Manning darted across the path toward the great hole in the wall. He pulled the pin to another concussion grenade and tossed it through the gap. Inside, a startled voice cried out. Manning heard the shuffle of boot leather as the enemy scrambled for cover or tried to reach the grenade to throw it back outside.

The explosion rocked the building and hurled a battered storm trooper through the gap in the wall. Bits of furniture and other debris accompanied the body. Manning swung through the hole and entered a severely damaged living room. The sofas and armchairs were covered with plaster dust and splinters. A wooden beam from the ceiling had fallen, shattering the glass top of a coffee table. One of the sofas was on fire, and flames crackled along the curtains.

Two more storm troopers lay among the debris. Both had dived behind a sofa for shelter. They were badly dazed, bleeding from ears and nostrils. Yet both were still armed. Manning couldn't afford to take any chances with the pair. He pointed his Uzi at the Nazi flunkies and squeezed the trigger.

The Canadian commando looked away from the bloodied, bullet-shredded bodies and glanced about for McCarter. The Briton had not followed him into the house. Manning feared his partner may have been hit by enemy fire, but realized it was more likely McCarter had simply entered the mansion from the open front door instead of through the jagged hole in the wall.

"Damn it, David," Manning hissed under his breath. "I said I was going in this way..."

Now the British commando and the Canadian ace were separated, and neither had the other to watch his back.

Automatic fire erupted in another part of the house. The sound could have been McCarter exchanging fire with the enemy, or Katz and James fighting Nazi gunmen at the rear.

Manning moved toward the sound, Uzi held at hip level. He stepped across mounds of fallen plaster and a long lamp that had tipped over. The room was dusty and grim. The heat from the fires made the Canadian sweat freely. The flames were steadily growing and could present a new danger if he remained in the mansion long enough.

A figure suddenly appeared at the archway to a corridor. Manning glimpsed a youthful, pale face contorted with rage. The opponent raised a Beretta M-12 and screamed with lunatic fury. The Phoenix commando immediately threw himself to the floor and landed on his side. A flash streaked from the Nazi gunman's Beretta as he fired it in a long, uncontrolled burst.

Manning returned fire with his Uzi. He nailed the enemy gunman point-blank in the chest with a trio of parabellum slugs. The man fell backward, blasting the ceiling. Manning, suddenly feeling pain in his left leg, glanced down to see his pant leg on fire. He smothered the flames by rolling on the floor.

"Shit," he rasped as he rose. The leg hurt, but he barely glanced down at the charred cloth and blistered flesh.

There was nothing he could do at the moment except tolerate the pain as best he could. The burn wasn't deep enough to be serious, but it hurt enough to cause Manning to limp as he approached the corridor. He glanced down at the young gunman he had been forced to kill. The youth's blue eyes stared up at him without seeing.

Blood trickled from the dead man's open mouth. His pasty features seemed even more pale in death.

Manning recognized the corpse. He had met the youth at the restaurant of the Royal Inn. The dead man had been introduced to him as John Wilkens. His real name was Gerhart, and he was the son of Otto Weissflog.

DAVID MCCARTER HAD ENTERED the mansion through the front door and was surprised to discover the Canadian hadn't followed him into the house. Like Manning, he suspected what had happened. A failure in communications, he thought, and naturally blamed Manning instead of himself.

He found himself in the front hall, alone except for the corpse of a slain storm trooper. No one stirred on the stairs, but he heard the blast of a concussion grenade in another portion of the house. McCarter reckoned it was near the ruptured wall Manning had probably used as an entrance. He started to head toward the noise, but at the sound of footsteps, he moved to the side of the stairs and ducked under the run. His back pressed against the wall, he waited for whoever was coming.

Werner and Reinhard entered the hall. They wore tan uniforms, caps and swastika armbands. Reinhard carried, besides a Beretta subgun from a shoulder strap, a heavy wooden crate. The lid had been pried off, and gray metal torpedo-shaped objects were visible among the packing straw in the box.

Werner carried two yard-long pieces of pipe, each with a bipod and baseplate mounted at one end. McCarter recognized the objects as mortars. Obsolete by modern standards, the weapons were still capable of throwing explosive projectiles great distances. Apparently the pair had decided to use the mortars in a last-ditch effort against the tanks outside.

"That's really a dumb idea," McCarter announced as he stepped from behind the stairs and pointed his Uzi at the pair.

Reinhard, his back to McCarter, dropped the crate and slowly raised his hands. Werner turned to face the Briton. He allowed one mortar to fall to the floor, but held the other tucked under an arm like a shotgunner off to hunt pheasant.

Suddenly Reinhard whirled, ducked and grabbed his Beretta M-12. McCarter's Uzi snarled. Two 9 mm parabellum slugs slit open Reinhard's forehead and a third chopped off his nose at the bridge. Brains and blood gushed from the back of his skull. Reinhard's corpse hit the floor, the Beretta still locked in its fists.

Werner hurled the mortar at McCarter. The steel pipe struck the Briton's forearms and knocked the Uzi. McCarter tried to swing the gun back on target as Werner rushed toward him. The big German swung a roundhouse kick and jack-booted the Uzi from his grasp. Werner's thick arm slashed a cross-body chop at McCarter's neck.

McCarter ducked under the whirling limb and drove a hard uppercut directly between Werner's legs. The Nazi howled in agony. McCarter continued with a spearhand stroke under his opponent's right arm. The tips of the rigid fingers struck the nerve center at Werner's armpit. McCarter followed with a hook to the German's solar plexus.

Werner groaned and started to double up, but suddenly unleashed an unexpected back-fist to McCarter's face. The British ace staggered backward, his head throbbing. Werner charged him, reaching out with both hands, intending to grab the Briton, yank him forward and knee his groin for revenge. Then he'd break his neck like a twig.

However, McCarter was not a willing victim. He stamped a boot heel to Werner's kneecap and leaned away from his opponent's groping hands. He grabbed Werner's right wrist with two hands, twisted hard and jammed his thumbs into the ulna nerve at the back of Werner's hand. The pain in his wrist and hand caught the Nazi off guard. McCarter applied more pressure and twisted his opponent's arm to lock it at the shoulder and elbow.

McCarter yanked hard. The pressure at his shoulder forced the Nazi to bow forward. McCarter kicked him in the face. Werner's head bounced from the blow. Still holding the Nazi's wrist, McCarter chopped his free hand into the crook of Werner's elbow. The captive arm bent. McCarter pushed and tripped his opponent, sending him to the floor. The German landed hard on his back. McCarter swiftly stooped and grabbed Werner's right leg at the ankle and behind the knee.

Standing erect, the Briton stretched his opponent's leg. Then he stomped a boot into the bodyguard's crotch. The vicious blow to his already battered testicles was too much for Werner. He thrashed about on the floor in agony and passed out.

"I got to give you credit, mate," McCarter said as he gasped to catch his breath. "You had balls."

THE DOOR TO THE DEN STOOD open. Gary Manning approached the room cautiously, his Uzi ready for trouble. Inside the den Otto Weissflog was seated at his desk. The Nazi leader held up open palms to show he was not armed. Manning kept back behind the doorway.

"Is that you, Turner?" Weissflog called out. "I suppose that isn't your real name. That doesn't matter now."

"You're finished, Weissflog!" Manning told him. "You have one chance to surrender!"

"I know you can simply throw grenades into this room and kill me," Weissflog stated. "I also know it is over. I can't surrender, you know. A trial and prison? Not my style. It's best if I die as *der Fuhrer* did. This situation is similar to what Adolf Hitler faced in the end. He took his own life in the bunker in Berlin when he knew it was over."

"I don't really care if you want to shoot yourself," Manning declared. "Go ahead and do it, but don't think I'm stupid enough to poke my head around the door to watch."

"Hitler's wife died with him," Weissflog continued. "My wife is in the bomb shelter with the women and children. I sent my son to guard them. He wanted to fight, but I wouldn't allow it."

Manning was aware Weissflog's son was already dead, but he didn't tell the Nazi. Maybe Weissflog didn't deserve to be spared any pain over the loss of a loved one, but Manning didn't feel any need to deliver this grim news.

"So, if I may make a last request," Weissflog began. "Will you go fetch my wife and bring her here? I have a cyanide capsule for her and one for myself. I think we should die together."

"I think you're out of your mind," Manning replied. "I'm not going to help you kill your wife, you crazy bastard. There's been enough killing already."

"Just one more life needs to be taken," Weissflog corrected.

The shot startled Manning. He stood at the doorway and waited to hear another sound, then slowly peered around the corner. Weissflog was slumped across his desk, a Walther P-38 pistol in his right hand. Smoke rose from the muzzle. Crimson-and-gray ooze smeared the Nazi's hair and streaked the ink blotter on his desk.

"Jesus," Manning rasped as he stepped into the den.

He approached the desk, Uzi ready. Weissflog did not stir. Manning jammed the stubby barrel of the Uzi against the Nazi's hand to push the Walther pistol from limp fingers. He shoved hard and sent the P-38 across the desk to the floor.

Suddenly fingers closed around the frame of the Uzi. Manning stared into the face of Otto Weissflog. The red gel and gray globs were only theatrical blood and special effects. The son of a bitch had faked his suicide to catch the Canadian commando off guard.

A fist crashed into Manning's jaw. Weissflog slammed the Uzi against the desk, forcing Manning to release it. The subgun fell from his grasp. Weissflog drove both fists into Manning's chest, knocking him back into a wall. The Nazi sprang from behind the desk, an SS dagger in his fist. The six-inch double-edged steel lunged at the Canadian's stomach.

Manning grabbed the madman's wrist. He held the knife at bay with one hand and clawed at Weissflog's face with the other. The Nazi growled, then slammed a knee into the Canadian's belly. He slapped Manning's head, banging it against the wall.

Manning pushed Weissflog's jaw hard and grabbed the knife. He twisted the Nazi's wrist as if wringing out a damp washcloth. The dagger fell from open fingers as Weissflog hissed in pain and punched Manning's kidney.

The Canadian responded with a backward elbow-stroke to Weissflog's breastbone, then another to the chin. The Nazi recoiled from the blows and started to sag. Manning heaved Weissflog up onto his back, then bent forward. The Nazi sailed over Manning's arched back and crashed to the carpet.

Rolling, he tried to get to his feet. Manning closed in and swung a hard left hook to his opponent's jaw, propelling him across the room.

Hitting the wall, the Nazi whirled and yanked a cavalry saber from a sword display on the wall. His face a mask of fury, blood trickling from his mouth, his eyes ablaze with hatred, Weissflog pointed the long steel blade at Manning.

"You fight well," he declared, "but not well enough."

Weissflog slashed the sword in a cross-body cut. Manning threw himself back onto the desk to avoid the blade. He executed a fast back-roll and landed feet-first behind the desk. Weissflog cursed and leaned forward to swing the saber at the Canadian's skull. Manning ducked, grabbed the chair behind the desk and threw it.

Weissflog raised his arms to block the chair. Although the blow knocked him back three steps and his forearms stung, he held onto his sword. Manning moved from behind the desk and stumbled into the umbrella stand, making his burnt calf ache terribly. Manning glanced down and saw the walnut shaft of an Austrian hiker's stave near his hand.

Weissflog charged, saber raised high. Manning yanked the stave from the stand and lunged. The hiker's spike struck Weissflog under the ribcage. His saber lashed out and missed Manning's head by less than an inch. The momentum carried Weissflog forward into the side of his desk.

The Nazi accidentally shoved the spike in deeper. The tip pierced his chest and punctured his heart. Weissflog opened his mouth to scream and vomited blood across his tunic. He collapsed. Manning stepped back and finally managed to draw his Walther P-88 from shoulder leather. He didn't need the pistol. This time Weissflog was really dead.

It was over, Manning realized as he walked unsteadily to the desk to retrieve his Uzi machine pistol. Phoenix Force had completed its mission, and the Nazis had been defeated once more. They would return to Stony Man and report to Hal Brognola. Then there would be another mission. There always was.

As Manning gathered up his Uzi, he noticed a book on the floor. It must have been knocked from Weissflog's desk during the fight. The Canadian picked up the book and examined the cover.

"Yeah," he muttered. "That figures."

He tossed the copy of *Mein Kampf* on the desk and walked from the room.

**A treacherous tale of time travel
in a desperate new world.**

JAMES AXLER

DEATH LANDS

Time Nomads

Trekking through the blasted heart of the new America, Ryan Cawdor and his band search the redoubts for hidden caches of food, weapons and technology — the legacy of a preholocaust society.

Near death after ingesting bacteria-ridden food, Ryan Cawdor lies motionless, his body paralyzed by the poison coursing through his system. Yet his mind races back to the early days in the Deathlands…where the past is a dream and the future is a nightmare.

TAKE 'EM NOW

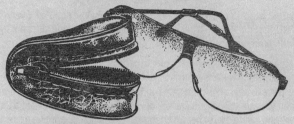

FOLDING SUNGLASSES
FROM GOLD EAGLE

Mean up your act with these tough, street-smart shades. Practical, too, because they fold 3 times into a handy, zip-up polyurethane pouch that fits neatly into your pocket. Rugged metal frame. Scratch-resistant acrylic lenses. Best of all, they can be yours for only $6.99.

MAIL YOUR ORDER TODAY.

Send your name, address, and zip code, along with a check or money order for just $6.99 + .75¢ for postage and handling (for a total of $7.74) payable to Gold Eagle Reader Service. (New York and Iowa residents please add applicable sales tax.)

Remove from pouch

unfold once

unfold twice

and they're ready to wear

Gold Eagle Reader Service
901 Fuhrmann Blvd.
GOLD EAGLE
P.O. Box 1396
Buffalo, N.Y. 14240-1396

GES-1A

Offer not available in Canada.

Do you know a real hero?

At Gold Eagle Books we know that heroes are not just fictional. Everyday someone somewhere is performing a selfless task, risking his or her own life without expectation of reward.

Gold Eagle would like to recognize America's local heroes by publishing their stories. If you know a true to life hero (that person might even be you) we'd like to hear about him or her. In 150-200 words tell us about a heroic deed you witnessed or experienced. Once a month, we'll select a local hero and award him or her with national recognition by printing his or her story on the inside back cover of THE EXECUTIONER series, and the ABLE TEAM, PHOENIX FORCE and/or VIETNAM: GROUND ZERO series.

Send your name, address, zip or postal code, along with your story of 150-200 words (and a photograph of the hero if possible), and mail to:

LOCAL HEROES AWARD
Gold Eagle Books
225 Duncan Mill Road
Don Mills, Ontario
M3B 3K9
Canada

The following rules apply: All stories and photographs submitted to Gold Eagle Books, published or not, become the property of Gold Eagle and cannot be returned. Submissions are subject to verification by local media before publication can occur. Not all stories will be published and photographs may or may not be used. Gold Eagle reserves the right to reprint an earlier LOCAL HEROES AWARD in the event that a verified hero cannot be found. Permission by the featured hero must be granted in writing to Gold Eagle Books prior to publication. Submit entries by December 31, 1990.